Silver Brumbies of the South

For Honor

Dragon
An imprint of the Children's Division
of the Collins Publishing Group
8 Grafton Street, London W1X 3LA

Published by Dragon Books 1968
Reprinted 1973, 1975, 1976, 1977, 1979, 1983, 1987

Copyright © Elyne Mitchell 1965

ISBN 0-583-30069-3

Printed and bound in Great Britain by
Cox & Wyman Ltd, Reading

Set in Intertype Plantin

ELYNE MITCHELL

Silver Brumbies
of the South

Text illustrations by Annette Macarthur-Onslow

DRAGON

South!

No cattle came to Dead Horse Gap that summer. No cattle roamed over the Ramshead Range. No red and white beasts with the wide-raking horns drank at the Crackenback River. Thowra, looking over from The Brindle Bull, knew that the time for the herds' arrival was past. Summer had come and there were no cattle. The mountains were quiet without them. No lonely, echoing bellow rang in the rocks, and the wild horses noticed the silence and the wind blowing over the empty hills.

If the mountains were empty of cattle, perhaps the men would not come either. Thowra, the silver brumby stallion, went one night past the silent hut at Dead Horse Gap to the Cascades. He was surprised, as he paced proudly down towards Yarraman's Valley, because there he heard a beast lowing. Cattle were at the Cascades but not in his beloved country – the country of the Crakenback, the Ramshead, and the great Main Range.

He stopped, one forefoot raised, silver ears pricked, nostrils quivering. There was only the whisper of the south wind in the snowgums and the far-away hoot of a mopoke. Again the bullock lowed, and the echo rolled and rang around the hills, farther, farther, dying in the distance, just as it had sounded for every summer of his life – when he was a foal running beside Bel Bel, when he was a yearling playing with his half-brother Storm, and in all his proud summers as the most beautiful brumby stallion ever to gallop across the Range. But no cattle had come to the high mountains this year. Something was different.

Men came out that summer, walking, measuring, taking sights, and before the summer ended, the silence of the mountains had been shattered by the sound, far down the valley, of blasting, and the roar of heavy earth-moving machinery. There were men: there was noise.

Miles away in the Secret Valley everything was still quiet. There was the sigh of swinging bark streamers, the movement of a possum, the sneeze of a kangaroo – no sound of men or machinery ever reached it.

5

At dead of night, in the star-struck darkness, Thowra would creep out of his Secret Valley, trot and trot long miles till he reached his river. Once there was the unknown, foul smell of oil in the waters of the Crackenback. It was that night that he climbed up to the free heights of the Ramshead Range and neighed his wild protest to the stars. Echoing, ringing round the mountains, the voice of Thowra sounded, but no one listened. The men in the camps might have turned in their sleep, but those who came to build roads had never heard of the Silver Stallion.

The mountains were different. The Silver Brumby could trumpet his great call through the night and no man would heed. Only the kurrawongs and gang-gangs would stir nervously where they slept, the wombats cease their food-hunting and look uneasily around them, the possums hide furtively in thick leaves. All that answered was the lonely cry of a dingo in the dark gullies.

Thowra went down, turned his head to the cool wind and trotted south – south, on and on through the night.

There were no horses at the northernmost end of the Cascades. Dawn was coming. Thowra broke into a canter, his tail, his mane, his forelock, flying free. He went bounding along in his immense strength, feeling sudden joy that drove away the uneasiness. Here he had claimed his first mare, the faithful Boon Boon, here he had fought and beaten other stallions. Here he was now cantering through the last, soft darkness. The light would come soon and his mane would be the crest of a silver wave, his tail a cascade of silver, and then he would hide in the trees: but today, perhaps, he would take no heed for safety. Did safety matter now?

He stopped and leapt on to a rock from which he had once challenged Arrow, when they were only foals, and from there he cried out his defiance – and exultation.

He waited, and the answer came, thin but clear – the call of his half-brother Storm. Thowra gave another great cry, for Storm and Storm alone, leapt off his rock, and went cantering on up the valley.

He had never known Storm and the herd of mares and foals to be so far south before. It was not till he reached the head of the Cascade Valley, in what used to be the country of that huge grey horse The Brolga, that Thowra found them.

The two stallions greeted each other in a half rear, necks

interlocked in mock battle. As they parted and dropped to the ground, Storm said:

"Hail, my brother of the wind and the snow: What brings you galloping through the dawn?"

Thowra did not answer, but asked a question himself:

"Why, O my brother, are you and the herd so far south?"

"I do not know," said Storm. "It is just a feeling that things are not right. Word comes through the bush and by the birds of the air that men, on foot, are everywhere."

"Yes," said Thowra. "And in the high mountains there are no cattle."

"There are cattle here," said Storm, "the usual stockmen came and left them, but there have been other men, wandering down from Dead Horse Gap."

"Along the Crackenback they make a track wide enough for six horses," said Thowra. "In the daytime there is a great noise. Benni, the kangaroo, told me, so I went out one day, and heard and saw."

Storm looked at him without understanding.

"A track wide enough for *six* horses!"

"Yes. They have cut it into the hillside, above the river, where once I ran from The Brolga and the men."

Storm raised his head and looked at the gap against the southern sky.

"Over there lie miles and miles of wild country. Other horses live there, and we shall have to fight for grass and an area for ourselves, but I think it is time to move from our own land. I may not go far, and perhaps may often return, but the young ones should go. What of you, brother? Surely your Secret Valley is safe?"

"Yes, though men on foot might find it more easily than men on horses would. I shall live there with my small herd, and I may still be able to roam the high mountains at night. I shall also come and visit you wherever you go. In my herd, you must remember, there is my son, Lightning – the Secret Valley is too small for him and he must find his own mares – there is a yearling now, too, Kunama's son. There are other foals and yearlings and two-year-olds of course, but those two are the wild and the free."

"What does Kunama call her son?"

"Baringa – for the light. He was born in a clear and brilliant dawn, after long dark days. He is silver and very finely

7

built. I think he may have inherited speed from Tambo. He looks as if he will go very fast."

"Tambo is pure racehorse," murmured Storm, "and you were never slow yourself."

"Lightning is not so fast, but no Secret Valley will hold those two."

"Well," said Storm, "perhaps the wild mountains to the south will be their country, just as this is ours."

"Tonight I shall go back to the Secret Valley," Thowra said. "Wait for me here. Then I shall go to the south with you – at least part of the way – and I may bring Lightning and Baringa."

It was evening when Thowra led Lightning and Baringa up the path from the Secret Valley.

Kunama watched them go. She was to foal again soon, so it was right that Baringa should go to this unknown land of the south without her. Tambo watched them too, and wondered if Baringa, who had the conformation needed for speed, threw to his sire whom he knew to have been a chestnut racehorse.

Boon Boon saw the three proud horses go too, realising their beauty, remembering Thowra leading his mares triumphantly down to the Cascades after defeating her sire The Brolga.

"There never was and never will be such a horse as the Silver Brumby was in his prime," she thought, but she looked at Lightning and Baringa, particularly Baringa. Baringa was so finely modelled, with slender, lovely legs, a deep girth, showing plenty of lung room, even though he was only a yearling, and a fiery, aristocratic head.

So they went, and so used were Boon Boon and Kunama to the Silver Brumby coming and going in and out of the Secret Valley that neither wondered if they would ever see the young ones there again.

"No hoofmark and no sound!" Thowra commanded, as they were coming near the top of the valley wall. "Remember, if you go back and forth from here you must move like ghosts, printless shadows without sound."

Lightning shook his mane impatiently. He had no intention of returning. He was a two-year-old. He had been forced by

8

his sire to stay quietly hidden for too long. True, Thowra had several times taken him to the Cascades, but he had had so little practice in fighting that he never succeeded in winning the filly he wanted. Now who cared if he was seen and chased by the stockmen! He would stay out: fight, win, make his own herd. His hoof knocked a loose stone which rattled as it fell.

Thowra turned and gave him a swift, quite friendly nip on the wither.

"The safety of all the mares and foals, not just the safety of your own hide, depends on our care. Mind how you go."

Baringa, the yearling, who was also trained in care and silence, but who had never been out of the valley, walked with nervous fire.

The dark night enfolded them, the bush hid them – this bush that hid wombats, kangaroos, wallabies, dingoes, possums, flying phalangers, all the sleeping birds and those who spent the dark hours in flight.

There was the faint, high squeak of a bat. Baringa shivered, but excitement made Lightning's heart beat fast and the blood pound in every inch of him. His silver coat tingled. He wanted to neigh loudly. He longed to prance and gallop.

The yearling came along silently, a thin wraith, a wisp of vapour in the night air.

Without looking behind him, Thowra knew that it was Baringa who floated over the ground, Lightning who made whatever sound they made. Lightning had been almost as difficult to teach the ways of those who will be hunted as Golden had been. Thowra doubted if Lightning would keep his freedom, but a colt of his age could no longer be kept in secret in a small valley with no mares of his own. If he, Thowra, did not take him out, he would go, like Kunama had, and possibly bring men searching for the place from whence he had come.

He quickened his pace, remembering the wild days when men hunted him through the mountains. There would surely be some excitement when there were silver horses in the bush again – two young silver stallions fighting for mares, leading all the other horses a mad dance, probably galloping from men.

Baringa felt the pace quicken, and sweat was soon wet on his coat.

Thowra led them through thick, rough bush across country, on a short cut to the Cascades.

"We will be there long before dawn," he said, and Baringa thought of resting amongst a shadowy collection of horses

9

who were asleep and half asleep beneath trees at the edge of the open valley. He did not expect to arrive into a herd that was restless and nervous, only waiting for the stallions to lead them off into unknown country, because, in the last few days, the horses had seen too many men. Baringa was surprised, too, by the stir in the mob when they appeared.

"Here he is!" the whisper went around. "Here he is!" as the Silver Stallion appeared among them, the king of the Cascades who had become a legend even to his own herd, even to the mares whose foals he had fathered, for he was there one night, galloping on a great spring wind, and vanished by morning.

There was a strange silence throughout the herd when they saw the two silver colts following him. Then the whispering started again:

"There are three, three – two colts from the Silver Herd."

Never in the Cascades herd had Thowra begotten a pure silver foal. He had got many creamies with dark points who rarely went free, for the men always hunted them, and he had got taffies, and some strangely handsome duns. Now the whisper went through the mares, the foals, the yearlings like St. Elmo's fire: "The Silver Herd, the Silver Herd." Magnificence, magic, mystery had come on the wind, horses they had never seen before, bred in secret, begotten on beautiful mares whom no one really knew – the silver horses who could arrive or vanish without sound or track.

These silver horses were Lightning, desperate with eagerness to fight the young colts and gather his first small herd, and Baringa, the yearling, tired and perhaps a little afraid of the grand new country he had wanted to see, and of the big herd of shadow horses in the night.

"You are here, brother," said Storm. "Let us move south tonight."

"South, south," came the insistent whisper from the herd. "Follow the Silver Stallion to the south."

Storm and Thowra drifted along together, grazing, walking, grazing, moving ever southward through the starlit hours of the night.

Beyond telling the two colts to stay close behind him, Thowra took little notice of them, but Baringa knew that he saw and heard every movement. Lightning, hanging back and straying from side to side, seemed unaware of this. Baringa was glad

10

to go slowly. He drank at a little creek and saw the faint reflection of his own head in the starlit water. He began to feel better and less nervous of looking around him. It was then that he realised that the horses that were closest to them kept on changing, as mare after mare came along to look at them through the darkness — as the braver colts and fillies ventured close and then dropped back again.

Suddenly he was bitten on the quarters. He whipped round and saw a bay yearling moving off. He looked at Lightning. No one seemed to have bitten him, but he was bigger and looked very strong. Probably no one would really molest them while they were close to Thowra — and while Lightning did not try to steal any of the young fillies.

The herd drifted upwards, through the trees, past starlit pools. Then the pools became smaller and smaller. There was sphagnum underfoot, and springs. It was the head of the Cascade Creek.

They reached a gap, Baringa knew, because suddenly the south wind came direct and cold, and because the stars seemed closer.

The two big stallions stopped. Baringa could see them sniffing the wind, and a tremor of excitement went through him. Through the night he saw the lightness of Thowra's silver mane flow and ripple in the breeze, and felt his own mane lift off his hot neck.

"The track does not drop straight downwards," Thowra said. "It seems to turn slightly east." He led off into thick bush along a faint, overgrown track. Once he looked back to be sure that Baringa and Lightning were following Storm. He did not want any trouble in the herd at this hour of the night and in a strange land.

Scrub scraped their flanks, branches of snowgums whipped their eyes, for they went along faster now, not stopping to graze since much of the hillside was rough and stony.

Lightning kept looking back, but he could only make out Baringa behind him. He imagined the long, winding line of mares with foals at foot, the young colts, the yearlings, the fillies. Back in the Secret Valley the herd would be sleeping beneath ribbon gums and candlebarks, safe, so safe, but here a herd of wild horses crept southwards into unknown country, which other brumbies owned. The sweat broke out on his coat with the excitement.

11

He knew that Thowra and Storm were walking much more carefully than they had before they left their own valley. So far there seemed to be no sign of other horses. Neither Lightning nor Baringa knew enough to wonder who had made the track – or who used it.

Thowra and Storm *had* seen signs of other horses, but these were only old droppings. Apparently no horses lived just near here.

Presently Lightning saw Thowra bend his head down for a moment, and from that moment he noticed a change in his bearing. He swung along with immense pride, as though enjoying the glory that was his.

Lightning, watching him, almost stumbled on a high heap of droppings. Another stallion came here! That was why Thowra walked with such pride.

The trees thinned out. The track turned slightly downwards. Light was spreading, filtering through the trees. It was day, and they were in strange country, the territory of strange horses.

They came out into open woods of large-boled, twisted, gnarled snowgums with fresh snowgrass underfoot. There were a good many tracks of horses about, none of them very fresh.

Thowra and Storm looked all around very carefully, trotting hither and thither, then put their heads down and began to graze.

The herd spread out, weaving silently through the trees.

Whiteface 'Plays Possum'

The ridge was not very wide and the trees were sufficiently open for Thowra or Storm to see a strange horse coming. The two stallions grazed, but they were watching all around them, listening for sounds, feeling with every hair. Lightning and Baringa, who were told to keep close, could see that they were on edge. Even the high piping of a tree-creeper startled them.

Baringa had never been in country like this before, with its rough, rugged hills and then the open snowgrass where the creek ran. The ridge would have seemed gentle if it was not that the trees looked as if they were perpetually beaten and lashed by the wind. At either end of it there was a high hill, and, beyond, to the south, a very high hill.

When Baringa saw Thowra grazing towards the eastern edge of the ridge he followed closely.

Thowra went to one end of the timber so that he could remain hidden by trees, and Baringa was so anxious to see what lay beyond that he came up alongside his grandsire and stood beside him, gazing over.

Never had he imagined anything like this. He looked out over miles and miles of blue ridges, some high, some low, each ridge deeply divided from the next by a creek or a river, till one ridge, higher than the rest, and far away, blocked all else from view. This ridge, itself, was deeply incised at its southern end by a gorge. There were miles of wild country in which even their large herd of horses would surely never be found.

They stood there, silver heads thrown up, looking far and wide through their camouflage of snowgum leaves. Then they both looked down to the country just below. Dropping quite steeply was a wide snowgrass valley flanked by ridges of thick bush.

Thowra stiffened.

Baringa immediately saw what had disturbed him. A mob of horses was grazing in the open, less than a quarter of a mile down the snowgrass valley. Thowra looked at them for a long time and then backed very quietly away.

13

Baringa did exactly as Thowra did.

"We needn't seek trouble yet. The blue stallion of that herd is about five," said Thowra. "We will move before the wind gets up and takes our scent to him."

Lightning was nowhere to be seen. Thowra's ears pricked back and forth.

"A sound will give us away," he said, more to himself than to Baringa, "and if that blue stallion and I fight, the mountains will know about it from here to the Tin Mines. *Where is Lightning?*"

Thowra, giving no appearance of haste, moved towards Storm. Soon he saw Lightning among some trees, rearing up in front of a young chestnut colt.

"One squeal and we'll have a fine big, blue stallion up here," Thowra muttered.

Just then a small, dun-coloured filly came up closer to the silver colt.

"That must be *my* daughter, not yours," said Thowra to Storm. "Lightning has no sense." He started to trot over towards him, but the chestnut gave a sudden scream of jealous fury and tore at Lightning.

Thowra swept in like a whirlwind and sent the young colts flying apart.

"You will have let the whole mountain world know we are here," he said, and even as he said it he wondered if it really mattered. He would fight the blue stallion and any other stallion that questioned their right to graze. What fun it would be! He went high-stepping back towards the edge of the ridge, head thrown up, proud and glorious.

Only the mares who had been in Storm's first small herd thought that Thowra and Storm might be ageing, but Thowra, of course, was magnificently strong. Did he not travel between the Cascades and the Secret Valley over and over again, and climb right up on to the Main Range just for the sake of joy!

The blue stallion was climbing up, up.

Thowra stood on the clear grass edge, shining for all to see, and ready to give battle.

On either side of him stood his son and grandson.

The blue horse was at a disadvantage, having to come up the hill, but it was quite obvious to Thowra, who had had to fight for his life so often, that he was cunning. He climbed slowly and rested often, also he climbed a little to one side of

14

the waiting horses, so that, in the end, Thowra had to move along to remain above him.

Well before that the three silver horses had seen that there was something queer about the look of the blue horse. Then as he drew closer they saw that his head was *white*.

"No wonder he is cunning," said Thowra. "With a head like that he'd have to be!"

The blue horse was heavy. He did not look as if he could move fast, but Thowra knew that his appearance might be deceiving. Any horse that looked as strange as that would have had plenty of experience of fighting.

Whiteface screamed his anger as he came slowly up.

Once Thowra's challenge rang out, and he listened with pleasure to his own neigh echoing off unknown mountains. Soon every brumby would know that there were silver horses out on the range again.

Baringa was starting to sweat with excitement. Both young horses backed a little as Whiteface drew closer, and as Thowra began to dance lightly on his neat, hard hooves.

Whiteface, by suddenly galloping, tried to get on to the ridge before Thowra reached him, but Thowra leapt along and down on to his opponent, and got in the first fierce strike.

Whiteface could fight – he had had to – but Thowra was enjoying himself enormously. This was life again. New country. Grass to be fought for – and the owner of the grass taught a lesson! He reared and struck, pivoted, struck, slashed with his teeth, struck and struck again – and always kept the other horse moving.

He gave a shout of rage as Whiteface slashed his neck. He leapt in and ripped the other's shoulder. He danced around him and bit him on the other side, he goaded the blue horse on and on.

After a time Whiteface began to tire. Thowra landed him a tremendous blow on the stifle – one that would lame him for a day or so when it stiffened up. Steadily, steadily he wore the blue horse down till he could only stand shaking with exhaustion, ready to be knocked over and pounded insensate.

Thowra stopped and looked at him. The big blue horse sank to the ground, completely exhausted. Once, years ago, Thowra had left another horse lying exhausted on the ground – the great, grey Brolga – but that time he had gone as a conqueror and claimed The Brolga's mares. This time old Whiteface

15

could have them, he had enough on his mind!

Also he wanted to stay around until old Whiteface recovered. There were things he might learn from him.

Lightning had other ideas. He sauntered down to look the herd over, knowing enough of the laws of the wild horses to realise that these mares were now, by the right of victory, the possession of his own sire – if he could continue to keep them. Thowra did not appear to be interested. He, Lightning, would risk his father's fury, and see if there were any pleasing-looking fillies.

As he drew near, he saw that he might have some trouble. There was a grey colt, almost as old as himself. This colt had been some distance off from the mob, and now it started coming towards him.

"Well," thought Lightning, "I want to learn to fight, and this looks like a lesson coming." Then his eye fell on a red roan filly in the mob. There were no red roans in Thowra's and Storm's vast herd. He would fight the horse and claim this filly! Perhaps he would just go up to the filly first.

He walked with swinging stride towards the herd, trying to emulate Thowra's proud carriage.

The grey started to trot.

Lightning could walk very fast, and a fast walk looked more dignified than a trot.

He reached the red roan filly just before the grey reached him – and forgot the grey.

He extended his silver nose to her trembling red-bay nose. Suddenly he squealed with excitement.

Then something had him by the withers – teeth biting in and in. He swung round to try to free himself and saw the grey's shoulder and forelegs.

He swung the other way. Still he could not free himself. He thought that the other must be going to kill him.

The herd watched with interest. Lightning was slightly bigger and stronger than the other colt. If he had gone for the grey instead of going to greet the filly and letting the grey attack first and get the grip that usually took hours of fighting to achieve, the silver horse should have beaten the grey very quickly.

At last Lightning became aware that his opponent was not strong enough to do anything but hang on – painful though that was. He tried to think how he could dislodge him.

16

He danced around for a second or so, then threw himself to the left, came back and up in a rear, striking round towards the grey, and roaring with rage.

The young colt's jaws were getting tired. His teeth slipped, tearing Lightning's hide.

Lightning managed to get his head between his knees and kicked up his heels with all his might, throwing the grey off at last. He gave a squeal of triumph.

Thowra, who had glanced down several times, snorted with impatience. A son of his wasted time and breath by squealing!

However, Lightning thought he had breath to spare. He rushed at the grey, striking furiously. The herd gathered close. Lightning squealed and tore around, kicked and struck and slashed, then squealed again.

Thowra, up on the ridge, watching Whiteface open one eye and shut it again, sighed and thought he would have to give Lightning a *lesson* in fighting. Whoever had heard of such a thing? But, of course, who had ever heard of a colt being hidden away in a secret valley till he was two years old? He surveyed the crumpled heap of blue horse again. It was time Whiteface recovered and looked more intelligent, but obviously the queer-looking beggar was playing possum. Thowra put his nose down closer to him and snorted hard.

Whiteface nearly jumped out of his ridiculous skin, and shut his eyes even tighter.

Thowra waited a little longer, trying to remember all he had ever heard about this country. The Tin Mine area he knew was supposed to be splendid grazing, open, and a long way from anywhere. Here he could not be far from the Jacobs River and the Moyangul – almost between the two, he thought. He had caught a glimpse of The Pilot on beyond. It was above the Tin Mine, and somewhere here was Suggan Buggan. "Suggan Buggan! That's the place for this stupid-looking horse," he thought, and bent down again and bit him on the ear.

Old Whiteface gave a horrified squeaking sort of whinny.

"Get up!" Thowra said, "and talk some sense – and if you don't talk sense I won't leave you alive! Now tell me, and tell me truthfully or that blue hide of yours won't be worth a gumnut after a gang-gang's finished with it, what lies between here and the Tin Mine – clear country or bush, good feed or no feed, and how many herds of horses?"

"I only know what I hear," said Whiteface sullenly.

"I know you're cunning," Thowra said. "You'd have to be, with a face like yours, but don't try to be cunning with me. *What* are the messages that the kurrawongs cry as they fly on the south wind?"

"What are you doing here, anyway?" Whiteface asked.

"It is quite possible for me to knock you over and finish you off if you don't answer my questions."

"Well, Silver Horse who travels by night! I know that there are many horses, many, many horses. There must be grass. There is a great flat they call the Quambat. . . . This is my country, and here have I stayed. . . ."

"This *was* your country," said Thowra. "My herd will graze here, at least for a while." He looked down the green valley and saw that the young grey colt had given up. Lightning had cut the filly out of the mob and was bringing her along near the fringe of trees. "I will leave your herd in peace," said Thowra, "though perhaps I might just go down and *see*." After all, Whiteface was not to be allowed to forget that he was beaten.

Whiteface snorted with anger, but found he was already stiffening up, and could hardly move.

Thowra went high-stepping down the soft grass slope. He passed fairly close to Lightning, who was leading his little red roan up towards the main herd.

Storm watched both horses, thinking with amusement — and pleasure — that the mountains were certainly going to ring with the noise of fighting for some time, now there were silver horses about. . . .

Three Horses of the Silver Herd

Storm did not wish to go very far from the Cascades, and this country of Whiteface's was big enough to hold both herds, at least for a while, but Thowra, now he had set forth for the south, was filled with a fever to go on and on — also, he might find somewhere for the two young silver colts to run safely in that wild and distant southern country.

One night, in the heavy darkness, Thowra moved from Storm's side, nipped Baringa on the shoulder, nipped Light-

18

ning, and told them to follow. Lightning woke the little red roan filly, Goonda, and she went too, just as she had gone everywhere with Lightning since he had fought for her and won her. The three young horses trembled with excitement and nervousness as they moved off through the night, leaving the herd behind them.

When they had gone a little way, down towards the Moyangul River, Thowra stopped and turned to the filly.

"Goonda," he said, "for fire were you named, and I know that the fire which men light is rarely silent, but if you come with the silver horses you must learn to be absolutely quiet." Yet he did not feel that it mattered much. They would be ghost horses, but they would be joyous marauders too. The mountains were going to ring with their names for a while, and if life got too dangerous then they could go into hiding again.

He did have a feeling that Lightning and Baringa might never want to go into hiding again – not till they had been almost caught a few times, or till they had a herd of mares in foal and with young foals at foot. A safe life was a boring one.

Anyway who should worry? It was night time. They were off to the south, to new country, and even old Whiteface had said nothing about men, or about brumby hunts.

When they got on to the brumby track in the timber Thowra began to trot along, only stopping occasionally to sniff the air and listen. Ahead he could smell the wonderful scent of mountain ash and knew there must be quite a forest of these enormous trees ahead of him. Where there was mountain ash there was never much food for horses, but there were the great trees through which one could dodge and play – or escape from enemies.

Before they reached the ash they found a small, swampy flat.

Thowra slowed up and sniffed the air. He could smell horse, and the night was still very dark. He walked slowly forward in complete silence.

The two young stallions were immediately behind him. They knew almost as soon as he did that something – some*one* – was in front of them.

Then there was a tremendous squeal, and it was as though the black night itself had leapt on them. With flailing hooves and snorting breath, an enormous black horse sprang on to Thowra.

The young horses shrank backwards, step by step, out of the

way. Thowra made no sound. After the first blows he leapt silently to one side, swung round, and sank on to his haunches. He could not see the horse – who undoubtedly had been able to see him a little – and he waited till bared teeth or the white of an eye might gleam in the darkness and show him where it was.

He could hear heavy breathing and could gauge fairly well where the black horse stood. He kept his own breathing so light that no one would hear it. At last he thought he knew the distance he must jump to land above that heavy breathing – what fun to hurtle through the air and fasten on to the neck or wither of that black horse!

He sprang off his haunches. His forefeet struck flesh. He sunk in his teeth and hung on.

There was a whirling black horse striving madly to be free of him. Thowra smelt the hot coat, the sweat, the blood, felt the fury of the horse whom he held in his strong teeth. He shook him and shook him. It was superb to be alive, to be out in the mountains again, to be fighting!

An amazing tussle went on through the last hour of darkness, but as the grey light came creeping, Thowra had exhausted the big black horse and he led his young horses on into the depth of the forest where the Moyangul River ran.

How strange to fight a horse in the night and barely see him, Baringa thought, shivering slightly, but Thowra went on and on, his head held high – proud and gay – the silver mane rippling and catching the pale light that filtered down through the great-trunked trees.

They went through the Moyangul River at a crossing that was deep in tea tree. Horses must have crossed there often. Thowra studied their tracks in the faint light.

Lightning gave Goonda a friendly nip. She had been very anxious to come with them (and he had had no intention of leaving her behind, now he had her), but she was a little nervous.

Baringa pawed at a ripple that caught the faint light in the sky, but he made no splash. At present he was much more afraid of making a noise than Thowra was. Thowra, after the years of being careful, was not really going to give a hoot for man or horse – but, of course, it was unlikely that there were any men out after horses yet.

It seemed that Thowra was intent on having a wonderful

time. Perhaps when he had made the mountains ring with his name he would go back to his Secret Valley.

They went trotting on through the mountain-ash forest, into which light began to slide as the sunlight flooded the sky, and they were enfolded in the lovely sharp smell of the leaves.

There were often tracks of horses, but no sign that any horses lived in the forest. This was a highway from one brumby bimble* to another.

Thowra went more cautiously as the track turned downwards through candlebarks and ribbongums, and became wider and more worn. Then, from the fringe of the trees, and in the glittering early morning, when the dew still diamonded the snowgrass, they saw for the first time a lovely, flat, open valley of the southern country – a wide valley, with shining water meandering through it, and low worn-down, timbered hills flanking it on either side.

Here was wonderful grazing for horses, wonderful, endless snowgrass on which to gallop.

Thowra stopped and gazed, and then his eyes searched the whole area for the herd that must live there.

One small herd was grazing right out in the open not far along the valley. Farther still he could see quite a number of horses scattered over the valley. A sparrow hawk sat on a great granite boulder, watching them, then it flew up and up in widening circles. Baringa felt sure it intended to see everything that was going to happen – for surely Thowra was going to fight by night and by day as they went southwards in the mountains.

Thowra watched the small herd for quite a while. He saw that the stallion was a big bay, slab-shouldered and rather ugly, saw that this horse kept a very strict eye on his mares – which meant that there were a lot of horses around. As he looked along that lovely valley, all shining in the early morning, Thowra felt gloriously alive.

He said nothing to his son and grandson, and they followed in amazement when he flung his head in the air and gambolled from side to side as he cantered down the slope.

Baringa, who had learnt all Thowra's and Kunama's lessons in bushcraft and silence far more thoroughly than Lightning had ever been bothered to do, was horrified when Thowra leapt

* An aboriginal word meaning the area owned by a tribe

21

on to the hawk's boulder and neighed loud and long. The cry echoed to the silver-blue sky, round the rolling timbered hills, along the flat, wide, green valley where the sky was reflected in half a hundred little pools.

Every horse raised its head to see who had called out joy and glory, and they stood staring, unbelieving, though already they half expected to see him because they had heard the whispers going through the bush . . . "the Silver Brumby" . . . "*three* silver horses" . . . Now here he was!

Then Thowra sprang off his rock and went cantering along the valley.

"If that bay stallion lets us," he thought, "we will feed here before we move on. If he tries to stop us, then I will fight."

They got well past the herd, then dropped their heads to graze, little Goonda in a sweat of exertion and fear, the young colts really too excited to eat, and Thowra with one ear cocked and one eye always on the bay stallion.

The stallion watched for a while and then came sauntering over.

Thowra went on grazing. The bay rushed at him furiously. Thowra jumped to one side and the bay hurtled past him.

"Is this grass all *yours*, that I cannot eat in peace?" Thowra snorted.

The bay did not answer. He thought to himself that he was a younger horse than Thowra and a better horse than Whiteface, whom Thowra had just beaten. He swung round to attack, and found Thowra standing in a half-rear, his eyes looking at him steadily and scornfully.

The bay paused and then rushed in. Thowra seemed to gather himself together and sprang. He was no longer in the same place, and the bay had not touched him.

The bay came for him with greater care this time. Once again Thowra vanished, untouched, from underneath his flailing hooves.

Soon Thowra had the slab-shouldered bay dancing all round him but never reaching him, and never a blow did Thowra, himself, strike. It was as though he had set out to mock this great, heavy horse, and defeat him without even so much as kicking him, simply by wearing him down.

Lightning and Baringa watched, even Lightning fascinated by this swift-moving, teasing battle. The Silver Brumby was going to add another legend to his name – that he could fight a horse, exhaust and defeat him without ever touching him.

There were young horses watching in the fringe of the forest, and when the big bay stood dripping with sweat and beaten, and then crumpled and dropped in a heap, these young ones went sliding off through the timber with a strange tale to tell.

Thowra grazed quietly and drank a little. The grass was sweet, the water fresh and good.

The bay horse's mares stood in a tight little group some distance away. Lightning kept looking towards them.

"We will go and see them," said Thowra, "but there is only one good-looking mare among them. His own fillies are slab-shouldered like himself, and would not travel fast enough for us – so don't dream of bringing one with you."

Lightning reflected that Thowra seemed to miss very little.

"The mob farther along the valley look to me to be younger, though it's hard to tell, so far away," Thowra went on, "but we are going to travel many miles, and I'll not be cluttered up with slow or ugly fillies. Goonda can travel well enough," he added kindly, because, after all, it had been necessary to make his victory over Whiteface a real victory.

"There were some young horses in the forest close by," said Baringa. "They crept up when the fight started, and went when the bay stallion was beaten."

Thowra looked at Baringa with surprise. It was a pleasure to have one of the colts prove himself capable of observing something that he had not first pointed out!

They were a beautiful pair. Baringa might have brains too!

Lightning surveyed the fillies with regret. A two-year-old should have a herd of more than one filly, and this was a strange way to travel, however, perhaps it was also quite exciting to be one of three silver horses.

Thowra found a nice rolling hole – probably the bay's – and rolled and rubbed the sweat out of his coat, then rolled in the snowgrass until he was clean and shining again. After this was over he turned his eyes up the valley.

The mob were all looking his way, heads thrown up.

"Come along," he said. "We'll see what happens next."

He set off at a canter up the flat valley floor. It was Goonda, trailing along behind, who realised what a magnificent sight they were, the three silver horses cantering with manes and tails flying free. For the first time pride in being with them rose above her nervousness. This was going to be a great deal more exciting than being in her father's herd.

Up the valley the mob of horses still stood nervously watching them, but as the silver horses grew close, panic seemed to seize them, and they turned and fled.

Thowra stopped to look around and to sniff at some rolling holes.

It was then that they saw with amazement two huge emus stepping and swaying their way into a side valley.

Thowra had been far too well trained to gallop after them and frighten them. Each bush bird or creature was someone of importance, Bel Bel had taught him when he was a foal, and he had tried to teach these young horses the same respect for every living thing in the bush. Now they had to keep their burning curiosity under control and not go direct to those long-legged, long-necked, swaying bunches of feathers, but to trot one way and back another, till they got close enough for Thowra to speak with the courtesy due to such noble, if shatteringly strange, birds.

"Hail, O noble ones," said Thowra, striking an attitude in which he himself looked noble, to cover the embarrassing fact that he did not feel completely certain that they were indeed birds. Obviously they could not fly!

"Hail, Silver Horse!" replied the larger of the two. "Your prowess goes before you, also the mystery of whether you are or whether you are not."

"We see for ourselves," said the second emu, "that you do, indeed, exist."

"Are you," asked the first, "the Silver Brumby, or the Silver Brumby's son?" And he peered with his small eyes, above the rather dangerous-looking beak, from one horse to another.

"I? I am the wind," said Thowra. "I come, I pass, and I am gone."

The strange feathers moved up and down, the strange voice said tartly:

"And are your sons the same?"

"My son is the lightning that strikes through the black night. My grandson is light that pierces the dark sky at dawning."

"Ah," said the first emu, "and we know your daughter is the snow that falls softly from above and clothes the world in white. You want but the rainbow – that is and was and never will be, and is yet the promise of life – and the glittering ice

24

which is there and is gone: then you and your family will possess all magic."

"It shall be," Thowra murmured. "And now, O noble ones, what can you tell us of this land to the south?"

"Nothing can we tell you," said the birds, "for all that you learn yourself is yours for ever. Go south like wind, and light, and lightning, till the south is yours, just as you made the Main Range yours."

"As wise as the owls," thought Thowra with some annoyance. "I don't suppose they've ever been to Quambat."

But the emus went on:

"The stone chimney of an old house, hollow-sounding ground and a weird hole, parts of a winged silver bird without feathers which fell from the air . . . and horses, horses, horses." Then they started to walk on. "We'll see you again," they said.

Thowra, wondering just what they meant, knew they would not say another word.

He looked around him very carefully before moving on, and as he gazed at the snowgums and candlebarks on the ridge close by, he slowly saw the form of a horse, hidden by branches and leaves – but there were the eyes, one ear, one nostril, some neck and black mane, a little of one bay shoulder shining, and one black foot, some of the bay back, some of the rump. It was a big horse and there was something very familiar about it, so that Thowra had to stop himself going to greet him with joy. He reminded himself that they were miles south of their usual country. He started to graze as though without purpose, but went in the direction of the hidden horse.

When one thought about it, of course, he and Storm had had many sons and daughters who must have spread over the mountains, some to live, wild and free, some to be caught by men. This horse, he felt sure he knew and remembered.

As he went closer, the horse came out of his leaves and branches, with confidence in his own strength, but with a friendly appearance – a big, noble bay.

"Greetings, O Silver Horse," he said.

"Greetings to you, first-born Son of Storm," Thowra answered.

The pleased expression on the big bay's face made him look even more like his sire.

"I heard tales that you were out on the Range again, that
25

you had already defeated three stallions, one without so much as touching him," he said to Thowra, "and for the sake of friendship between my sire and you I wished to greet you."

"Well said, Son of Storm."

"Stay a while here with us and share our grass," said the bay. "My herd is not far off." He raised his head and called. "I came south for grass and a bimble of my own, and here I stayed where the grass was good, and where I could gallop and enjoy myself, here, in this valley, and over on to the head of the Ingegoodbee River."

"Do men ever come?" asked Thowra. "We have seen cattle."

"Oh yes, they bring the cattle out, and come to salt them. Sometimes we have to gallop for our lives, but they do not worry us much. Years ago there used to be men working the Tin Mines, and there are huts and a fenced paddock, on the Ingegoodbee, where the stockmen sometimes sleep."

Quietly stepping out of the trees came a herd – about seven neat-looking mares and half a dozen foals and yearlings – to whom Thowra gave ceremonious greeting, introducing Lightning and Baringa and Goonda to them all. Among them was a filly, more than a yearling, light chestnut with silver mane and tail, a direct throwback to Yarraman, sire of both Thowra and Storm. She and Baringa played together. Lightning thought:

"She is too young to follow us now, but I will remember her."

They grazed with the herd nearly all day, but at evening, as the cool south wind sprang up, Thowra said farewell and Son of Storm spoke as Storm, himself, might have:

"Here I will be," he said, "and perhaps someday I may be of use to you, or your son, or your grandson. Do not forget."

"We will remember," said Thowra, and once more they set off for the south, while pale sunset clouds hung in the light blue sky of evening, and there was a softness over the wide valley, the red in the candlebarks was burnished, the water reflected the blue and pink of the sky. All the country (in fair weather) was gentle, old. In wind and blizzard this south country could also be hard and wild.

Soon they crossed the low gap and were on the head of the Ingegoodbee, in an even wider, swampy valley with still, reflecting pools. One wild duck winged its way across the quiet evening sky.

26

There was the fence. Before long they could see the slab-and-shingle huts. Thowra stopped with forefoot uplifted and ears pricked, but all was silent. No smoke came from the chimneys, there was only the mournful evening cry of a kurrawong in the snowgums.

Quambat Flat

A network of brumby tracks wound through the bush west of the Ingegoodbee, and everywhere there were the big heaps of droppings that tell a traveller – horse or human – that this is a country where there are many, many brumby herds.

It was almost night before Thowra and his silver colts left the Tin Mine camp, and they went away quietly, filled with the queer loneliness of the old empty huts – the slab walls through which the evening breeze crept, the rotting shingle roofs, the old smell of tame horses, and the frightening smell of men and of their fires.

The two colts had never seen men. They had never seen a

high-fenced round yard, but Thowra made them go into the one by the old feedroom so that they would know that a horse could be yarded and caught.

Baringa sweated with fear because he could imagine what it might be like to be fenced in. Lightning flexed his muscles.

"No man will ever catch me," he thought. "I will gallop, swift as lightning across the sky." He did not look back as they left, but Thowra and Baringa both turned for a last glance at that strange loneliness of the bush, empty tumbling-down huts, where only the wind moves.

Then they went nosing on through the trees until they found a very well-defined brumby track heading almost directly over the ridge, westward.

Thowra travelled quietly now. Occasionally he felt himself sweat with excitement, knowing there were many horses around.

A wombat was sitting near his hole, another grubbing around for grass. Thowra had noticed the great number of wombat holes, now he stopped to try to get information.

"Greetings, O wombat," he said. "Have you seen other horses go by just lately?"

The wombat looked up out of its very small eyes.

"Horses, horses all the time, eating all the grass, galloping in the moonlight – but they have heard you are about, and the young ones are on the move."

"What older stallions are there?" Thowra inquired.

The wombat looked at him and at the colts without speaking, but after a while he said:

"I do not know where you have come from, because it is years since tales of your beauty and speed went through the mountains. You are indeed handsome, but why are you here, where you never ran before, bringing wild excitement to the other horses?"

"The cattle have left my own country, and men make a hard, wide track along the Crackenback River. Men walk even to the Cascades, so we come south."

"Men come here sometimes, but never have I known excitement go through the brumbies like fire through the bush, as the excitement that goes ahead of you, O Silver Horse."

Thowra thought it sounded as if there might be some fun, and also knew that the wombats were not going to answer his questions. He and his colts and the one little filly went on very quickly through the bush. When they came on fresh brumby tracks they all felt a throbbing current of excitement flow through them, and they began to walk in complete silence, placing their hooves on tussocks of snow-grass rather than the bare earth of the track.

Goonda, feeling the excitement flowing from one to another, did her best to place her small hooves where Lightning placed his.

The solid darkness of a night without a moon closed in around them as they went.

Suddenly Thowra was sure he heard or felt quite a number of animals moving on either side of him. They were silent movers too, because he could barely hear them. He stopped to see if they would stop. The faint following noise ceased, but he was still aware of another presence. He moved on. The faint sounds started only a second afterwards – so he, too, could be heard, and possibly seen.

He began to feel conscious of every silver hair, conscious of the colts behind him. He stared through the darkness.

Yes. He could faintly see things some distance off through the bush on each side, and, farther back on the right, the blurry outline of a mare who must be lighter coloured.

His interest quickened. They were being paced by quite a herd of horses, and the mare was no filly, but fully grown, and perhaps beautiful.

He strained his eyes through the night, but there were only shadows and half sounds. Then they were near the verge of the forest and coming to the other side of the ridge.

Thowra stopped as the ground began to drop below his feet. He waited, but the other horses did not move. He moved a little down the hill. They moved too. He stopped and they stopped. At last he decided to go out into the clear, wide valley below. There he would see them more plainly – not just the hint of a horse in the night.

The stallion of the herd must be big, strong and confident, since he had not hidden away from the silver horses as every other brumby around the Tin Mine seemed to have done.

Walking proudly ahead of the two colts, Thowra went down into the valley.

The other horses did not come.

Thowra led his little company well out into the open, and there they stopped. He could tell that Baringa was very excited, by the speed of his breathing. Lightning was beginning to get bored and restless.

"Lightning will never have the imagination to be one jump ahead of an enemy," thought Thowra. But who was one jump ahead of *who*, at the moment?

A possible faint sound from the north made Thowra lead his colts off the track southwards. They walked a little way and listened, walked and listened.

The night held only the sound of crickets in the wet grass and, from far down the valley, a plover's cry came sadly through the dark to make the sweat go cold on a horse's back.

"We are alone again," thought Thowra.

They came to the creek and he put in his nose to drink, stopping in sudden surprise because the water ran the opposite way to that of the Ingegoodbee. Then he drank quietly.

They walked up the creek some distance before he found a place where they could jump across without sending muddy water downstream to any waiting horses.

Thowra could have given a few bucks for joy, it was so exciting to be out at night in completely strange country, and country where many horses ran! The other stallion was probably even now waiting for him near where the track left the valley and went up the hill into the bush. Well, blow the other stallion!

He led his small herd right to the foot of the hill and then turned towards the track and crept along, just for the fun of it, and because he was curious about the herd that had paced him almost as silently as he, himself, could go.

When he knew they must be nearly at the track he turned and nipped each of the others to tell them to stand still. Then he went on alone, almost floating over the ground, silently, silently, and close under the hillside, so that he would not show up by starlight. There was the wonderful old feeling of every nerve-ending tingling. How grand to be creeping up on other horses again, with the familiar stars to watch him, and unknown mountains all around.

The stallion must be there. He stood quite still. He was sure there were horses close. He stared and stared through the darkness. There was the shape of the light-coloured mare beyond some bushes! He also saw a silvery tail swishing beside her, and could not really see the horse.

He went slowly forward, quite close, though there were still some bushes between them. Then he stopped, threw up his head, and gave his tremendous call:

"It is I, Thowra!"

The air seemed suddenly to become alive with movement, and there was a roar of rage, or triumph, or surprise, or even fright!

Thowra sprang out from behind his bushes. He could see the mare and several others moving back in the darkness. He could see the shadowy outlines of a stallion who must be a dark grey.

This dark grey was big. Would it be possible to defeat him without striking a blow? Thowra decided not. He waited for the other to attack.

The big grey eyed him for some seconds.

"What do you here, Thowra?" he asked at last, and his tone was not friendly.

"Much the same as you do, I suppose," answered Thowra.

The grey snorted.

His mares were coming up quietly behind him. He turned and stamped his forefeet at them.

Thowra could easily have sprung on him at that moment, but he simply stood looking proud – and perhaps disdainful. He could see why the dark grey stallion sent his mares back: the pale-coloured one, even in the dark, had the possibility of being beautiful.

"They speak of the Silver Stallion as though you are magic," the big grey snorted again, "but you are only a fool. Go on your way to the Quambat, or wherever you are going."

Thowra had had no intention of adding to his herd, but the grey had asked for trouble! Quick as a flash Thowra replied:

"I go to Quambat, but your pale mare comes with me."

He let the grey spring first – dodged him, gave him a thundering, maddening whack as he went past. Every blow Thowra struck after that was calculated to infuriate rather than damage, and the big grey horse got angrier and angrier and fought stupidly.

Thowra seemed simply to slide away from under each blow after it touched him.

After a while the grey made a big effort to fight more carefully and win, but Thowra was a great fighter – perhaps the

31

greatest fighter the mountains had ever known – and this grey had called him a fool!

Thowra intended to exhaust him, but he also intended to give him a few marks by which he would remember this fight. He did not hurry. The stars had moved a long way across the sky by the time the big, dark grey was exhausted, and beaten. As the grey gave in, Thowra became aware of a large number of horses watching, and also of the fact that Lightning was fighting a young stallion quite close to the pale-coloured mare.

Thowra stepped proudly over to the mare. The other horses melted away from around her – except the two young ones who went on fighting as though no one else existed. No notice was taken of the young ones brawling. All eyes were on the proud stallion.

"Come," Thowra said to the mare, nipping her gently on the wither. Then he led off along the track to the Quambat followed by Baringa and the new mare.

Goonda stood trembling, and then decided to follow. She called Lightning loudly and clearly, and he, horrified at the thought of being left behind, gave his opponent one last whack with his forefeet, and rushed after the other silver horses.

Thowra asked the mare if she had ever been to Quambat, and she answered with pride that she came from there. He found out that if they kept trotting along at the pace they were going the stars would certainly not have faded from the sky by the time they got to Quambat Flat.

"I would rather arrive at daylight," said Thowra. "We will rest for a while when we next come to water."

The kookaburras roared out their dawn laughter as the silver brumbies, the little red roan and the big, light grey mare slid through the trees and stared out over the Quambat Flat. There was utter silence for a moment and then a magpie caroled, another took up the song, and the kookaburras started to laugh again.

A faint mist curled up from the small creek that flowed down the centre of the wide flat. Several lots of horses were grazing. The magpie song filled the air, and now there came the double warble of a red-tipped pardalotte.

Thowra started visibly as he saw a stone chimney, all that remained of a hut. Who had said "a stone chimney"? The

32

emus, of course. What else had they said? "A winged, silver bird" was one thing.

He moved slightly farther forward so that fewer trees spoilt his view. It was a big flat, and, except for a small tongue of bushland between two arms of the creek, it was clear. He looked up at the mountains on the opposite side, the rugged, rock-topped Cobras, and then let his eyes slide slowly over their bush-covered flanks and back to the flat. Once again he jumped with surprise. In the bush lay something like an enormous silver bird.

"Those emus!" he thought. "Perhaps they *have* been here." Whatever it was that lay in the bush, it did not look as if it would hurt them. They also had said "hollow-sounding ground, a weird hole, and many, many horses".

As he watched, another three or four horses stepped out of the trees near the silver bird. Then he noticed, down the flat where it narrowed, a group of young horses were playing in the shining mist. Lightning and Baringa watched them too.

At the top end of the flat, among some trees, there was a tall, light grey stallion, with dark points, and a mare almost exactly similar.

Thowra surveyed the whole flat, shining in the mist and early sunshine, and said to the two colts:

"If you've got any sense you'll make *this* your kingdom. I made the Cascades mine."

He started to walk slowly through the trees down one side of the flat.

The young horses still played, still shone. The mist wreathed upwards, glittering to meet the glittering sun, and a young white filly seemed to leap up, dancing in the dancing mist. Others joined her to rear and leap, and their colours were all intermingled, but Thowra and the colts had all seen the white filly.

As they watched her they nearly fell into an enormous hole.

"Those emus!" said Thowra, as though it was the fault of the emus that the huge hole existed − or their fault that he, Thowra, was looking at a filly playing rather than where he was going!

It *was* a weird hole, grassed all over, as if it had simply sunk. Six or eight horses could easily have fitted into it, and its sides were not too steep to go up and down. Thowra went very

33

carefully round the edge, his nose curling suspiciously, then walked on, through the trees at the side of the flat.

He stopped quite close to the gambolling horses.

"I am going right round the flat keeping in the fringe of the trees," he said. He looked at Lightning, who was looking only at the young horses in the shining mist, then at Baringa. Baringa looked from Thowra to the young horses, and back to Thowra.

"When I have had a good wander round I will return to the main herd," said Thowra, "and then to the Secret Valley. You must remember that the Secret Valley must always be secret. I will see you again," he added. "I will come back."

He went off through the trees. Baringa watched him with a strange feeling he had never felt before. Lightning walked out in the open, proud and lovely, towards the shining young horses and the white filly. Baringa followed him, still trying to see where Thowra had gone through the trees.

Thowra went off with the sudden embarrassing realisation that he had the new grey mare with him. He kept on going.

He saw the young horses chasing each other, and felt a great longing to race, himself, on that wide flat such as he had never seen before.

He crossed the creek, low down, among trees. A sacred kingfisher sat immobile on a branch above the water. As he got further round, below the Cobras, he could see a high mountain to the north, and suddenly knew it was The Pilot. He was indeed in a strange new land, far, far away from his home.

More and more he longed to gallop and roll on that flat, drink at the creek, cry out his joy to the wild surrounding hills.

He was stupid to have brought this mare, but she was beautiful. Well, with or without her, he would race down on to the flat and let all the southland know that he, the Silver Brumby, was here *now* – and then he would vanish.

He went right round the flat as far as the lifeless silver bird which, as the emus had said, had no feathers, but he saw that it could do nothing to him, and thought that the emus had mentioned it perhaps only as a proof that they had been there, perhaps as a promise that they would come again.

The grey mare did not even seem curious about it. She must have known it well. She had said very little, except to say where they should go, since they left the Tin Mine Creek, yet she looked no fool.

"Come," he said, and with stones and earth flying up behind his hooves, he galloped down into the middle of the flat. He galloped across to the creek and round, listening to the hollow sound of his hooves. Then he stopped, whirled around, and decided to roll.

He ate some of the sweet grass, drank at the stream. The feel of Quambat, the taste of it, the smell, were his.

The kookaburras were still laughing, a white-throated tree-creeper piped, high and clear. The light grey stallion and his mare came down, but the stallion was offering friendship, not fight. He had heard much of Thowra, both now and years ago.

"The bush rings with your name, O Thowra," the big, handsome horse said. "We heard tales of you many summers ago, and now you are here, still living, though we once heard you were dead. I know you do not fight to kill, I know you must return to your own mares soon. The Quambat Flat is yours while you are here – but what, O Thowra, brings you?"

"Men make roads in my mountains," answered Thowra, who liked the handsome grey horse. "It was time that our herds came away – and I, I just wanted to wander like the wind from whom I was named. I must go back to my mares, as you say, but I will return here, where I leave my son and grandson, O Grey of Quambat Flat. I thank you for your courtesy."

"Cloud is my name," the grey said. "This mare is Mist, the mare you have with you is my full sister."

"My name," said the mare, "is Cirrus. I too am a cloud. I suggest, O Thowra, that I remain here, with my old herd, a token by which the Quambat will remember you, and yours, when you return."

Thowra looked at her.

"Perhaps you have spoken wisely, O Cirrus. If I take you to my herd the other mares who have run with me for years will not be pleased."

"Here I will remain," said Cirrus. "You will remember me and you will return."

Silver Forest

Quambat Flat felt springy underfoot as Lightning, followed by Baringa, walked out of the trees. The mob of young horses looked wildly exciting. Lightning could go quietly no longer. He broke into a canter, jumped the creek, and was there, with the other horses, before they saw him.

The young things, who were most of them not as old as Lightning, gathered round the two silver colts. Soft, quivering noses were outstretched – grey, chestnut, blue roan, red roan, white, dun, bay. Some ears were pricked forward, some laid back. Some eyes looked at them with friendship, some eyes rolled and showed the whites. Then the chestnut colt squealed, swung round and kicked at Lightning. The whole mob galloped up the flat with Lightning, Baringa, and Goonda among them. They swung, they galloped back again, then round in a circle and propped.

Then off they went again, down the flat to the trees, back and around.

These horses, with the exception of the chestnut colt and Lightning, were really too young to fight properly, and though they might have a spiteful bite and kick at the strangers, that would be all, for as yet they had no herd nor country to possess and protect.

Then Thowra came down on to the flat with the greys.

Even the youngest of the horses had heard of Thowra: now they looked from him to Lightning and Baringa, looked and wondered, and stopped their play.

The white filly was near Baringa, grazing occasionally, watching him, watching Thowra.

Baringa had his head up. The little filly saw his ears flickering back and forth as though he listened for a call from the tremendous silver horse.

She picked at the grass closer and closer to Baringa, then raised her head a little.

"Is he your sire?" she whispered.

Baringa started nervously, but he saw that the one who spoke to him was the white filly, that she was beautiful and sweet-natured.

"He is my grandsire," he answered. "I am son of Kunama and Tambo. Lightning is his son, full brother to Kunama."

Lightning was grazing his way towards her, unmindful of the chestnut colt who was running with the young mob though already almost mature enough to have mares of his own.

The white filly moved closer to Baringa, till she was almost touching him.

Lightning came nearer and extended his nose towards her, but just then the chestnut cantered up and bit him on the neck. In a flash Lightning was after the chestnut, or the chestnut after Lightning, in a half-spiteful game.

"What is your name?" the little filly whispered, her head close to Baringa's, as he dropped his nose for a half-hearted mouthful of grass.

He looked up at Thowra again.

"Baringa," he answered. "I am named for the light."

"They call me Dawn," said the white filly softly.

After a while they saw Thowra say farewell to the two greys. The big silver horse looked down the flat towards the young ones, and Baringa started forward as though in answer to a call that had not come, but Thowra turned away and went towards the bush, and northwards.

Baringa dropped his head to graze, he looked dejected. Presently the white filly, Dawn, gave him a playful nip on the shoulder and went prancing off, leading him in a gay gallop through the creek, then on, up through the trees on the northern side of the flat.

Sometimes she reared up on her hind legs, sometimes kicked and danced sideways, as though she were only playing, but she was steadily going in the direction in which Thowra had gone.

Lightning and the chestnut colt were squabbling and did not miss them.

Presently Dawn stopped.

"If you want to be with him so much, why don't we keep following him? You must know where he is going."

"I know where he will arrive, in the end," Baringa answered, "but he will go without track or sound, a ghost through the bush."

Dawn trembled with excitement, and she felt her hair rising. How exciting to follow a ghost horse.

"Come along," she said. "Let us go together. We may find him, and it will be fun." She did not say that she would like to get away from both the chestnut and Lightning, for soon they would be fighting in earnest. The arrival of the silver horses had, in a moment, made both the chestnut colt and the white filly grow up.

She danced along through the forest in a northerly direction – white light dancing – and Baringa followed.

They soon found the brumby track along which Thowra and the colts had travelled that morning. There was no single track going back along it.

"I told you he would leave no track," Baringa said. "Nor will we! Come! I will show you!"

He led her through the bush parallel with the track, putting his neat hooves on grass tussocks, never bare earth. For the first time since Thowra had left him, he felt confident, strong, and completely part of his surroundings. This was something he could do – move without sign or sound through the bush. He led the lovely, shining filly as if she were his.

At first he looked back often, to be certain that she placed her feet exactly where he had put his. She was following with grace and certainty.

On and on they went, and he began to feel better. The filly and he went well together. He could feel her following, moving exactly as he moved. He would not miss the Secret Valley and Thowra and Kunama so much if he and Dawn could roam wild and free together.

They came to a creek and drank, his cream nose and her white nose close together in the ice-cold water. As he raised his head to let this lovely water trickle down his throat, he noticed that Dawn's mane and tail were silver, like his.

They went on. Baringa was getting tired – he had been travelling for two nights and two days now. Also he had a feeling that Thowra might not go through the Tin Mine area in

38

daylight, as the country was so open, and that if they went too far they might miss him.

He found a dense patch of tea tree and a little clear ground inside it, on which they could lie.

"We will rest here," he said, "and go on in the dark."

The flicker of Dawn's ears was all that showed that she was excited.

It was almost night when they moved again, and they had not gone far when Baringa suddenly dropped his nose to the ground, looked very carefully, sniffed.

There was the faintest hoofmark – and it was Thowra's. He went on with even greater care. Ahead was another tea-tree thicket. He crept forward and knew that Dawn was creeping exactly as he did. It was difficult to get through this tea tree without letting a branch rustle or fly back with a swish.

Inside was another little clearing, and there was Thowra, standing flexing every muscle ready to set forth for the night's travelling. Then his ears twitched because he heard or felt something.

Baringa moved into the clearing, silent as a wisp of mist, Dawn following him.

"Baringa!" Thowra greeted him with outstretched nose and a gleam of amusement and respect in his eyes. He had been right: this colt had brains too! He had found *him*, Thowra! Also he had got the lovely little filly!

"What is it, Baringa?" he asked. "What do you want?"

"Only that I wished to be with you."

"Listen!" said Thowra. "I hear someone else!" He stood with trembling ears and nostrils.

Baringa and Dawn both strained their ears to hear any sound. There was a faint thud, thud, thud.

They waited.

Presently two kangaroos, a buck and a doe with a joey in her pouch, hopped into their small clearing.

Dawn was amazed to see Baringa's expression of joy, and to see him stretch out his nose, which the buck kangaroo immediately gave a friendly box with his small front paw.

"Benni, O Benni," said Baringa. "What brings you so far from home?"

The kangaroo folded his paws neatly and bowed his head towards Thowra.

"Greetings, O Thowra," he said. "We heard that the

39

stallions of the Silver Herd had gone south, and we, too, decided we would see what sort of land lay this way. Even before we left, great noisy machines were walking up the track the men have made. It is time to find new grazing."

"Take heed, Baringa, to what Benni says," Thowra said gravely. "Benni has ever brought warning of what goes on in the mountains, to me and to your mother also. Take heed, and now that I have led you safely to the south, make this country your own. Learn where to graze and where to sleep. Learn every hiding place, every place for escape, and learn it before the men know you are here. I have promised to return to see you, and when you are older and know all that you must know of this country – and can fight for, and hold, that lovely filly – you, too, may sometimes visit your old home."

Benni nodded wisely, then gave a gigantic sneeze.

"We will see you also, Baringa, and if ever you are in danger we will try to help. Come back south now, and roam far and wide."

"Farewell till our next meeting," said Thowra. "Farewell white filly; farewell, Benni and Silky." He touched Baringa's nose, then faded into the darkness and the tea-tree scrub.

Benni boxed Baringa's nose again as the young colt stood gazing after Thowra.

"Come on," he said. "Perhaps we four – five counting our daughter – might make our way up on to the Pilot Mountain. I have been there once, long ago. It is a nice place for children to play," he said, giving the yearling another little punch on the muzzle, "and beyond it lies all that wild Suggan Buggan Range, that would hide a hundred horses." Then he looked at the filly. "My name, as you will have heard, is Benni. My wife is Silky . . ."

"They call me Dawn."

"Well, Dawn and Baringa, shall we go?"

"Yes," the two young horses said eagerly.

"Good," said Benni. "Now, you two will be very quiet and leave no track."

"Yes," they answered again.

On, on through the night the odd company went, the kangaroos bounding, the colt and filly trotting along. They came to a lovely glade where a creek headed among star-flowered heath.

"Here the grass seems very good," said Benni. "We will
40

graze here for a little while. Above us the mountain becomes very steep. Tell me, Baringa," he went on, "had you found the Silver Brumby in the night, or did you go with him from the Quambat?"

"Oh, we found him."

"Ah ha," said Benni. "Learnt your lessons better than he expected!"

"What do you mean?" asked Baringa.

"Never mind."

Baringa listened to the night as he grazed. The sounds were those that had been familiar always – a cricket chirping, the croak of a frog, a faraway hoot of a mopoke, a possum crying "quark", the rustle of a wombat moving through the under-growth – but now he must hear everything and know what each sound was, in case there was a warning of danger to Dawn and himself.

There was one sound that came occasionally and seemed to be getting nearer. It sounded like something grazing its way through the bush, *and stopping and listening as it came*. He nudged Dawn and led her into the trees and undergrowth at the opposite side of the glade from where the faint sound came, whispering to Benni as he passed:

"Listen. Something comes."

"You are right," said Benni. "*We* are in no danger. We will stay grazing to see what it is."

Baringa and Dawn slid in amongst the bushes and then crept carefully and slowly along beside the glade, remaining well hidden. When they were right at the top of the glade, they waited and watched.

Baringa felt the drying sweat making his coat cold and stiff. He should not be afraid because Benni was there, Benni who had once warned Thowra of a great manhunt, and who had led Kunama out of danger.

The sound came closer and closer, though it was still barely a sound. Whoever made it knew something about creeping silently. Then, into the glade came the shadowy shape of the big, dark grey stallion who had fought Thowra at the Tin Mine.

Even in darkness Baringa could tell that he was angry, also that he was lame.

Head down, he followed their scent about the glade. They could hear him sometimes drawing in his breath through

41

dilated nostrils. He was so intent on the scent of horse that he nearly fell over Benni.

Benni gave the coughing bark of a kangaroo in anger, and the horse jumped backwards.

"Do you never look where you are going?" Benni asked sharply.

"I was intent on following a scent," the horse replied, somewhat ashamed, because everyone knows that the mountain kangaroos are harmless, gentle, courteous creatures.

"What scent did you follow so intently that it overpowered mine, O grey stallion?"

"I heard from a half-sleeping jay that two young silver horses went past not long ago. I will have no silver horse in my country!" The great grey shook with anger. "Where the silver horses run, men soon come and there are great brumby drives."

"True, O grey stallion," Benni said, "but you are sure that you are not eager to catch the blameless colts because the stallion beat you last night?"

The grey horse snorted with fury.

"Young or old, I will not have them. I would surely kill, rather than have silver horses running here."

"Thowra defeats his enemies without killing! If he hears that you have threatened to take the life of his young son and grandson *your* life will surely be in danger," Benni spoke very gravely.

Baringa, listening, knew that Benni was threatening the stallion, but also playing for time for Dawn and him to escape. Once more he nosed Dawn, and they turned and crept away. Silky was ceaselessly hopping round the glade, thumping with her tail: Benni was talking. Between them they would cover any sound the young horses might make.

Baringa tried to stop being afraid because Thowra had taught him that the sweat of fear smelt very strongly.

He moved silently between bushes, under snowgum branches, past their knotted boles, stepping quietly, quietly, and the hair of his hide told him that Dawn followed close.

They went straight upwards, up and up, towards the bare top of The Pilot, the rocks and the stars. After they had been going some time, and there was no sound of following hooves on stones, Baringa's fear began to turn to that sort of perilous, marvellous joy that is contained within danger.

At last, from the movement of the air, and because the trees were becoming very small, they knew they must be getting near the top, where all winds could blow.

"I do not think anyone is near," said Baringa. "We can risk going beyond the trees and right up over the rocks to the top. We must be quiet, though."

They left the last trees behind, and the wind lifted their manes off their hot necks. There were just the rocks above them, the top of The Pilot, the stars, the sky, and the wind.

They tested each rock with their hard hooves before they put weight on it. Up, up, they went, almost touched by the stars.

Baringa would not have been grandson to Thowra if he had not felt fierce exultation at being out in space, on a mountain thrust high against the sky. He stood trembling on the top, Dawn beside him, flank to flank, staring out over the darkness that hid miles of bush and mountains – and wild horses – and he could have cried out then: "Here am I, here am I!" but he must be silent, in his new found strength and joy.

After feeling the wind and the distance and the height flow around them for some time, they turned, getting cold, and walked together down the back of the rocks till they found the first twisted snowgums.

"A little further," said Baringa, "and we will have better shelter. There we will wait for Benni and Silky and also for daylight, and we will see where we are."

They found trees and rocks where they could shelter, and stood close together for warmth, half sleeping, and waited for the kangaroos.

"How is it," asked Dawn, "that these kangaroos are your friends?"

"They warned Thowra of danger, years ago, and then my mother, when she was a foal, had few others to play with except the wombats and kangaroos, and Benni loved her very much. He has been my playmate too. He will come soon, but he will not hurry because of Silky and her joey."

"Is Lightning friendly with all the bush animals, too?" Dawn asked.

A cold, creeping feeling of discomfort went down Baringa's back.

"Yes," he said slowly, "but Lightning . . ." he stopped. He did not want to say that Lightning was impatient and thought a great deal of himself, but he did want Dawn to like him the

43

most. He wanted Dawn to follow him through the bush always.

Dawn nipped him gently on the neck.

Baringa wondered whether Lightning might not be very angry with him when he returned. He supposed Lightning might easily consider that he should just remain with him, as a yearling, in whatever herd he collected, and that he, Baringa, should not go off with the lovely white filly. . . . Perhaps The Pilot might be a good place . . . if there were water. . . .

After they had slept an hour or so they heard the thud, thud of kangaroos hopping.

"Here they are," said Baringa.

Dawn jumped nervously, being more sound asleep than Baringa.

Baringa walked out to greet them.

"My thanks, O Benni, for holding that horse in talk, and you, Silky, for making a noise round the glade while we escaped," he said, putting his nose down to each kangaroo.

"Your thanks are nicely said, my Baringa," Benni replied, "but we ever help the Silver Herd, O grandson of Thowra. You heard what that horse said?"

"We heard."

"Well, remember! For that grey would indeed kill you, Baringa. He would kill you for being one of the Silver Herd. We might not always be here, so, until you are full grown, take care!"

Baringa shivered, standing there on the top of The Pilot before daybreak.

"I will take care," he said.

"I think," said Benni, "that the grey is Steel, son of the great, grey stallion, The Brolga, who defeated Thowra's father, Yarraman, when he had grown old, and whom Thowra, himself, defeated to become king of the Cascade brumbies. This horse is barely any younger than Thowra, and he would remember. He would be an enemy – to the death – of any of the Silver Herd."

Baringa felt warm again because he had remembered the glow and fire of danger.

"Life seems dangerous," he said cheerfully.

Benni tapped him playfully on the shoulder.

"For any silver horse it is, but Lightning has one less to worry him. He need not fear you . . . yet," he said, then he added: "Son of Storm is to be trusted."

44

Baringa looked thoughtfully at Benni, and found himself wondering again what his reception was going to be when he got back to Lightning.

The first grey light came at last, and then the silver rays of the sun touched the rocks, the low, weird, wind-tormented trees, the kangaroos grazing on the glittering green grass, the silver colt and filly.

"This is a strange, exciting place," said Benni.

"Why does it look like this?" Dawn asked. "I have never seen such trees."

"It is high, and there is no other sheltering high ground near it. Heavy snow comes in winter, and the north-west wind blows nearly always. See how the trees are blown out towards Suggan Buggan? They look like a horse's mane blowing in the wind, don't they? Come, we will go along the ridge a little way."

He and Silky started to hop quietly along. Sometimes they stopped to nibble grass, the lovely curves of their grey backs in contrast to the thick, gnarled bole of a snowgum whose branches had never grown to any size. Then the kangaroos would sit up again, balanced on their big grey tails, and go off in rhythmic bounds after the dancing horses.

The ridge dropped down slowly. Green glades wound among lichen-covered granite outcrops and the twisted trees. The grass was very good.

Occasionally they came upon the signs of horses, but nothing to show that any stallion had recently lived up there. The bright sun began to have warmth and life in it. The young horses galloped up and down the glades and round and round the kangaroos, silver manes and tails flying.

The ridge was flattening out. Baringa stopped short in a gallop because the living trees, just suddenly, in a straight line across the ridge, became dead trees, stark and white. Limbs that had been twisted by the wind when they were living, still now, stiff and dead, streamed fantastically in a wind which was not blowing.

"We could run through this and never be seen," said Baringa. "Our legs would look like the limbs of bleached trees, our manes would blow in the wind as the trees once blew. It is our forest."

"They have died in the shape into which they were blown when they were alive," said Dawn.

"Yes, but we are living," Baringa bucked around among the bleached, wind-streaming trees.

"A fire must have come through, many years ago, and killed these trees," Benni said, "so long ago that the charcoal and black scars have been bleached and worn off by sun and wind, rain and snow."

"A fire!" said Dawn.

"What is a fire?" asked Baringa.

Benni looked at them in surprise.

"You are so young that you have never seen a fire!"

"What is it?" Baringa asked again.

"You know the burning heat of summer," said Benni. "Sometimes there is not much rain and snow in winter, then the next summer is hotter than ever. There is no water in springs or creeks. The grass is dry, the leaves are dry. Heat is everywhere, shimmering, burning heat. There is smoke in the air."

"I have seen and smelt smoke," said Dawn.

"Then wind brings the red flames to eat everything, to burn and burn. There is no grass, no air to breathe."

"And it leaves death?" asked Baringa.

"It leaves death," said Benni. "The bones of kangaroos and horses."

"Thowra has never mentioned this fire to me," said Baringa.

Benni looked surprised.

"Even Thowra may not have lived through a fire," he said. "I am older than Thowra. I have seen fire. Come now," he said. "Silky and I must go and find a sleeping place for the day, but before I go I would like you to look all around you so that you know where you are, in what directions the rivers, the ridges, the valleys lie."

"What a long way there is of rough bush," said Dawn, looking over the Berrima Range, over Suggan Buggan, right away over ridge after ridge towards where the Snowy River ran.

"Yes," said Benni. "Wild country into which the cattlemen do not go much. I think a horse could escape from men fairly easily there, but come and look westward! To the south lie the Cobras, above Quambat. You've seen them. To the west lies the wild, steep country that drops, and drops, and drops, oh so far, down into the Murray Valley." Then he added slowly and thoughtfully. "There might be some deep and secret places there."

46

Young Horses at Quambat

Baringa was too young to be alone with Dawn in the mountains, too young to protect her, too young really to look after them both if the weather became very bad, though now in sunshine, and with all the good grass on The Pilot ridge, they were safe and happy.

Then the kangaroos went on farther south, and, each night after they left, the young horses felt very much on their own.

Late one day, as blue, cold evening crept up from the valley, they started to drift towards the Quambat, towards other horses.

It was dark when they got there. They knew, from the scent, that horses had been there all day and were sleeping in the trees close by, but they made no sound, and no one discovered them till morning.

Lightning was quite pleased to see Baringa, though he had been too busy fighting to bother about him much. He had only just managed to keep Goonda with him — more because all the young horses exhausted themselves than because of any skill in fighting.

He had learnt a good deal.

The light grey stallion, Cloud, did not worry the young horses. If he noticed them fighting he did nothing about it, but lived each day serenely in the sun.

Lightning saw Baringa quite early in the morning. He neighed to call him over. He did notice that Baringa only walked over slowly, but did not think that the yearling might be nervous of his reception, or that, after a time of being proudly on his own, he was feeling young and small again, compared with his splendid uncle.

Lightning's neigh, of course, drew attention to himself. The other young horses were all fresh after a night's rest, and ready to annoy him. The chestnut came trotting out, followed by a couple of other colts, a dun, a blue roan.

Baringa retreated into the bush with Dawn as they all started to rampage around Lightning. Lightning enjoyed the fighting and the play. It was only play now, but soon they would be fighting — this time it was the dun who struck at him

47

fiercely. The other two drew back and watched, and then started to fight among themselves.

Lightning felt proud that Baringa would see how he had learnt to fight in these days since they got to Quambat Flat. He arched his neck with its silver mane, and knew he looked very grand. He had not fought this dun horse before and he soon began to realise that he seemed to be an experienced fighter.

Lightning got a cutting slash from the dun's hooves on his shoulder, then felt blood running. He was hurt for the first time. He reared up and tried to smash his hooves down on this horse who had hurt him. For the first time, too, he felt his own hooves cutting into flesh. But he had used too much strength and could neither rear up again, quickly, nor leap out of the way, so that the more experienced dun seemed to heave himself out from underneath, and fasten on his neck.

Lightning shook him off and swung round to get a savage kick into him. Then he saw the chestnut near Goonda, and he tore after them in a rage. The dun followed and they all fought each other until they were exhausted.

After a long drink at the creek, Lightning and Goonda moved towards Baringa.

It was then that he saw Dawn with Baringa.

Walking slowly, because he was already stiffening, he greeted both Baringa and Dawn with ceremony and grazed beside them for a while, then nipped Dawn gently on the shoulder. She turned quickly and bit him. He circled round her and tried to drive her into the trees.

Suddenly a fury of lashing hooves was upon him. Teeth tore at him. A maddened piece of quicksilver fastened onto his neck, then swung and kicked, leapt and struck.

This was Baringa! He must have learnt too!

Lightning was startled. He was so exhausted that he did not realise that Baringa was not very strong.

Baringa stood looking at him with high pride and courage. He relaxed a little when Lightning lay down and rolled.

The two silver colts had been brought up together. It was natural that they should graze close to each other. Lightning simply stayed with Baringa, trying to seem as if he had not meant to make Dawn his.

He asked Baringa where he had been. Baringa was rather quiet, he did not even tell Goonda what he had seen and done.

48

He kept close to Dawn, and neither of them went far from the trees.

The big dun came striding up once, but Dawn bit and kicked every time he came near her and both the colts were ready to attack him, so he went off to a safer distance.

Baringa realised that in one way he had more chance of keeping Dawn if he were near Lightning, but at the same time he could not trust Lightning. He would have to learn to fight very well himself. Each day made him older and stronger, but each day made Lightning older and stronger too, also the big dun, and the fiery chestnut who was so swift to attack, but perhaps stupid.

So, day after day, while the two-year-olds battled till they were tired out, Baringa played with the yearlings and fought mock fights with them. There was not a yearling whom he could not quickly outdistance in a gallop, not one whom he could not dodge and parry, in a fight, until they left him alone.

Baringa and Lightning both learnt.

Lightning still had Goonda as his only mare. He knew that the most beautiful filly of the Quambat was Dawn and felt that she should be his, but he still remembered Baringa's swift, flashing fury, and did not realise that he had been so easily beaten by Baringa that day because he was already exhausted.

Baringa remembered Thowra's parting words to him, and he had not been back at Quambat many days before he and Dawn started wandering off on their own again.

The first morning Lightning woke and found them gone, he felt angry, and even angrier when he could not find their tracks.

Baringa and Dawn had gone up the creek, before the first light, slipping through the forest without sound or sign.

Cloud and Mist heard no one pass, as they slept in a small clearing. The big dun was among scrub bushes where the creek became little more than a knife cut. He neither saw nor heard them as they went creeping past, frightened that he would wake yet enjoying the thrill of danger.

It was in the big clearing at the creek's head that they found quite a number of other young horses and joined these for several days. It was here, too, that Baringa had his first fight with a horse older and bigger than himself – the heavy hooves pounding the ground, the hot breath from red nostrils

49

– and found that by dodging and dancing as he had seen Thowra do, he could at least survive.

The summer days became very hot. The bush smelt of hot dry eucalypt leaves, dry earth, dry kangaroo grass. Trigger plants made bright puce drifts in the grass. The tea tree was flowering in the creeks. The showy podolepis made fields of gold to gild the legs of silver horses. The pardalottes called and the kookaburras laughed. The sweet song of the grey thrush and the cry of kurrawongs blended together. This was summer, the long months in which young horses grow in the sun, in which, if they are wise, they wander about to learn all the hiding places of their own part of the mountains, all the places where the best grass and herbage grow. During this time Baringa became faster and faster and also swift and sure in all his movements. Lightning became a stronger and stronger fighter.

Baringa and Dawn explored far and wide. They always sneaked away without Lightning, who had forgotten Thowra's lessons in silent travelling. Baringa knew it annoyed him when they went.

Dawn realised that the young horses regarded Baringa as something unusual. It was not just his speed – the fact that he was far faster than any of them – but the mystery of his coming and going without anyone hearing him or seeing him, and his knowledge of the country so that he might dodge under a fallen tree, jump an invisible rock face into a creek and vanish from those that chased him.

Lightning was growing into a very handsome horse. He knew it when a strange horse with his two mares went past, and it was he, not the other young colts, whom the horse was ready to strike, and it was at him that the mares looked. He knew it, too, because he felt it in every inch of himself, from his neat hooves and strong legs to the tips of his silvery ears. He felt magnificent – and it was undoubtedly time that Dawn stopped running free with Baringa and joined his herd.

Baringa and Dawn were away, but he knew they would return, so he waited.

Then one morning he saw them not far away, among the candlebarks – half hidden by creamy tree-trunks.

"It is always as though they are there and yet not there," he thought crossly. It was true. More and more it seemed that Baringa and Dawn merged into the country. None of the young horses could know that Thowra, years ago, up on the Ramshead Range and in the Cascades, had made himself part of the land just as mysteriously. Lightning should have been like this too – and was not.

Feeling cross, feeling determined, and feeling strong and handsome, Lightning walked towards Baringa and Dawn.

He stood in front of Dawn thinking that she could not fail to realise his glory, and go with him when he called.

The two young horses looked at him curiously. Then he told Dawn it was time to go with him.

Dawn took no notice, but began to graze quietly off, away from him. Baringa stood still with anger.

"Why should you, so beautiful, waste your life running round the country with Baringa, who is little more than a foal?" said Lightning.

Dawn, again, took no notice, but Baringa looked different. The hardness and strength of anger that had been in his stance was weakened by sudden misery, as he wondered if perhaps Dawn really would like to run with the strong stallion.

Dawn just kept on moving quietly away. Lightning ran round in front of her again. She still took no notice, only changed her direction once more.

"Come!" Lightning said even more imperiously, feeling sure that she was only teasing, because how could she not want to go with him?

She looked round at Baringa, and gave Lightning an angry bite!

Lightning still thought she was leading him on, and tried to push her off in the direction he wanted her to go. She bit fiercely.

This time there was no mistaking that she meant it. Lightning was angry and was silly enough to show his anger as he tried to claim her interest and force her to go with him.

Through the air came the same silver fury that had attacked him before.

Baringa struck him a sharp blow by the ear, just as Dawn kicked. He turned round to go for Baringa. But Baringa was no longer there. The horse who was no more than a foal was already striking him from the other side!

Dawn and Baringa were thoroughly roused, Dawn protecting herself and Baringa filled with anger at anyone trying to take her away.

51

Lightning had his only flash of good sense for the morning. He knew it was time to get out.

He backed away hastily and tried to seem as if he had not meant anything at all.

This time Baringa was unlikely to forget. He waited an hour or so, until Lightning had moved a little distance off, and then led Dawn quietly away, up the creek where the kookaburras were laughing.

Lightning was watching them cornerways. He followed them. In no time at all he could not see a glimmer of light on their hides, no moving flicker of silver, and underfoot he could find no tracks, not even grass pressed down in the shape of a hoof.

They had gone, printless as a light breeze goes.

He walked on up the creek, with Goonda following. He had never been right up to the spring which was the source of the creek. Now he saw strange horses, like shadows, moving between the trees. These duns and roans of the southern country were good colours for hiding themselves, not like he was, with his shining hide.

There was still no trace of Baringa and Dawn.

A kookaburra, sitting on a branch, looked down its long beak.

"Searching for your brother, are you?" he said. "He and the little filly went on upwards, may be on to The Pilot."

So Lightning and Goonda went upwards too.

The bush grew very thick, dense, whippy suckers hiding fallen logs and tumbled-in wombat holes. They could not see where they were going at all. A branch swished Lightning across the eyes. A scissor-grinder mocked them. He began to go slower. Goonda was wishing he would stop and go back, but he kept on, though he was already beginning to feel the aloneness of the bush. He had never been away from other horses before except when he was led to the south by Thowra.

He went on and on, his beautiful coat becoming streaked with sweat. At last, when it was already late, the trees started to thin out and there was an open hillside ahead.

When they went out on to the rocky ridge, where the digger's speed-well was already flowering in long spikes of dark blue, he felt the cold touch of space, for the country was steep below them, steep into the misted gullies towards the Murray – and he, with the oblique sun's rays glittering on his pale coat, was a solitary silver horse.

Goonda's red roan hide made her unnoticeable.

Soon the rocks forced them off the ridge top. Either they must walk on that bare, stony hillside, without any cover, or give up, go back into the bush, and go down to the Quambat without Dawn.

Lightning went on, stepping more carefully so that he did not send rocks rolling and crashing down to attract attention, but he was far too unpractised to be good at walking quietly, so the noise he made was quite loud. He was horribly conscious of himself. He felt, with every step, that he must be a glittering silver horse for all to see, and his skin shivered and tingled all over.

He stopped quite often to look around to make sure there was no one near. He looked and he listened with quivering ears. Baringa must be somewhere, and there might easily be others: but he could see no one at all.

With every step he wished that he could give up without even Goonda knowing that he was beaten. Baringa and Dawn could really be anywhere. Should he say to her, in an offhand manner, that he couldn't see a sign of them, and home was a pleasant place?

Just then he felt himself turn to ice.

Above — and not far above — there was an iron-grey horse almost hidden in the rocks.

Steel!

Lightning felt his heart suddenly leap inside him. He stood absolutely still, frozen by fear. He wanted to turn and gallop, but he could not even move, and what a hillside to gallop down! If only he could vanish like Baringa seemed to be able to do, but even Baringa would not be able to vanish on this steep, open slope with rough granite all over it, and anyway Baringa would never be out on an exposed hillside, glittering in the sunset.

The iron-grey horse was watching him. Lightning could almost feel his eyes on him.

Slowly Lightning started to think again. If he did not want to gallop down this terrible hillside, the great grey stallion might not want to either. Perhaps if he turned round and walked, the other might only follow at a walk, perhaps he might be able to dodge him in the snowgums. Perhaps . . . perhaps . . .

He started to turn round very slowly. His eyes met Goonda's troubled eyes.

"That iron-grey stallion, Steel, from the Tin Mines," Lightning said. "Turn and go back the way we came – no faster than a walk unless I tell you."

His skin pricking with fear, Lightning walked behind Goonda. A sharp piece of granite pricked the frog of his off fore hoof. This would indeed be a terrible place to gallop. A loose boulder rolled with him, and he had to jump to save himself. The boulder went crashing down towards the great valleys where shadows were already gathering. As he listened to it, he thought he heard the sound of another rock above him. He tried to walk more carefully and turn round at the same time.

Yes, oh yes, that big dark grey was coming after them.

Lightning had never been frightened like this before. He was shaking, and the sweat began to run off him. If only he could gallop and gallop to the sheltering trees that were so steeply below!

Steel seemed closer!

"Faster, Goonda!" he said in terror.

Goonda was surefooted and light, but she did not like the idea of tearing down this mountainside. At his command she blundered forward, and Lightning leapt after her.

It would have been better to keep on walking. The big horse knew how to go fast over very bad, steep country.

"Faster!" Lightning called to Goonda.

The noise of their hooves and the bounding rocks which they sent flying was tremendous.

Baringa and Dawn were still in the dense snowgums, waiting for twilight before they went up to their twisted white forest near the top of The Pilot. They looked out, hearing the noise, and Baringa, horrified, saw that Lightning might just reach the trees before the grey, but he would have no second to spare – and what would happen in the trees?

Baringa waited till they were almost to the snowgums, then, telling Dawn to head up and over the timbered ridge on to the eastern fall, he walked out into the open, and, as Thowra would have done, leapt on to a rock and neighed loud and long.

54

Steel heard him, and then saw him poised – light, young, but full of the promise of magnificence.

Ahead was the tired and terrified Lightning: above, on the rock, was the other silver colt glorying in a future that was not yet his. Steel stopped in his headlong gallop and wondered which to chase first.

It was that hesitation that allowed Lightning to get into the trees.

A Mystery and a Secret

Lightning was too tired and frightened to realise quite what had happened. He knew he had heard Baringa, knew that Steel had stopped for a moment and then come crashing on. In that moment he and Goonda had got into the trees.

All he could think now was that he must go quietly and he might be able to hide and get away. Instead of tearing straight on he told Goonda to follow him, and turned on an upward line, as he subsconsciously went towards Baringa's last neigh.

He could hear Steel smashing through the suckers and fallen timber below them, still going straight ahead from where they had entered the trees.

When they came to some particularly dense undergrowth, he forced a way into it. The whippy snowgums closed up behind them, and they stood still, hidden, and able to take a breath.

Soon they could hear Steel returning and crashing around looking for them. He was coming their way. The sweat of fear broke out on them again. He was coming! Goonda and Lightning, terrified to turn their backs on the direction from which they could hear him coming, backed out of their thick cover.

Baringa did not seem to be anywhere.

Suddenly Lightning felt that the only thing to do was to try to get back to Quambat. If he could have gone to Thowra and the Secret Valley he would have, but that was just a far away paradise.

He changed direction again and crept along behind a thicket of hop scrub. He could still hear Steel breaking branches. Then, from a little farther above, there rang out Baringa's neigh.

55

Steel crashed his way towards the sound, and Lightning and Goonda crept on down, gaining a little, and also getting their breath back while Steel wasted his on furious searching.

Lightning had never crept so quietly before, but even so his foot knocked a rock flying down on to another one.

The noise it made seemed enormous. He hoped that Steel was making too much noise himself to notice it, but in a second he knew that Steel was after him again.

A little brown-coloured pigeon scurried away under some scrub. He heard a tree-creeper's repetitive whistle, saw it running up the trunk of a candlebark. Everything else was safe but him.

Baringa neighed again, but this time Steel knew in which direction Lightning must be and even Baringa's provocative call would not attract him.

Lightning and Goonda hid in some tea tree and stood almost without breathing while Steel went thundering around.

Baringa must have known where they were because his next call came from below and to the west. Steel swung that way.

Lightning and Goonda went on.

All the way back to Quambat they crept, in a grim game of hide-and-seek. Each time, just as it seemed that Steel must find them, there was a noise of another horse or Baringa's thrilling neigh: "It is I – find me!"

What could save them at Quambat? Lightning knew of nowhere to hide. Baringa might know caves, or hidden shelves above the creek, but Lightning did not. All he knew was that Quambat was home, and somehow he must get there.

They were edging round one of the little clearings when Steel burst through the trees, after them.

Lightning lost his head completely, and started to gallop. He half noticed, as he tore through the next clearing, some strange shapes by the creek, then a voice said:

"Go to Cloud! *Cloud!*"

Afterwards he knew it was an emu who had spoken, but at the time only the name "Cloud" went into his mind, and he raced madly on for the place where Cloud and Mist usually grazed at evening.

There they were, on an open, grassy place, just above the main Quambat Flat. They were already looking up as they heard the galloping hooves.

Cloud gave a trumpeting snort as he saw Steel coming hard

on Lightning's heels. He gathered himself together and, as the iron-grey was almost level, hurtled himself forward so that his broad chest hit the dark grey shoulder and knocked Steel out of stride and nearly to the ground. Then he reared up beside Steel ready to strike.

Steel managed to get his balance again and leapt off to follow Lightning, but a great blow from Cloud's off foreleg got him on the side of the head. Then Cloud was in front of him, and another blow had almost knocked him over.

Steel was very tired. He had galloped a long way in rough country, and in this state he had very little hope of defeating Cloud. It did not take long for Cloud to exhaust him, and when Steel stood shaking in every limb, unable to kick, or strike, or bite any longer, Cloud stopped and said:

"Take yourself back to the Tin Mines. If you disturb us here again you will surely die!"

"I will go," said Steel, "but why let these silver colts live here? Where they are, men will come, and there will be no peace in the mountains at all!"

"If I want no silver horses, then must I beget no more myself," Cloud answered furiously. "Now get you gone — coward that would kill a yearling or a two-year-old — or I, sire of Dawn, will surely kill you!" And he drove and harried Steel away along the brumby trail that led to the Tin Mines, until Steel collapsed, unable to walk another step.

Baringa had turned quickly back through the bush to find Dawn. The sunset lights were already fading around Quambat Flat, and clouds burning red and gold over the invisible Murray Valley. The kookaburras were laughing out their last laugh at the dying day. Night would come soon out of those mysterious clefts where the darkness already lay, and he must hurry if he were to find Dawn before the twilight had faded completely.

He was uneasy. Though their silver forest might hide them for a while, it was no hiding place for the space of new moon to old moon, or from snowfall to spring, or even for the spring-time mating season. It was time he and Dawn found a place somewhere, out of sight of Steel, of the big dun, and undoubtedly of Lightning. Tomorrow they must start because they could no longer run with Lightning. Even if he, himself, had, by distracting Steel's attention over and over again, saved Lightning from a fearful beating, he knew that he could not trust Lightning again. Until he, Baringa, was old enough and strong enough to hold Dawn for himself, Lightning would always try to steal her. Between himself and his dam's full brother there might never be such friendship as there always had been between Thowra and Storm – because there was Dawn.

Baringa hurried on now, up and up, as fast as he could go without making a noise. He was also wondering where he would find Dawn, how he would find her if he dared not call.

The light was beginning to fade even from the sky when he saw her coming towards him, almost gliding over the dark ground, between dark trees.

They touched noses and rubbed each other's withers, there in the thick forest of night, and then Baringa led her back up The Pilot, till they reached their silver forest. The south wind blew strong and cold, so they moved on to the western slope where they found some rocks that still held the warmth of the sun, and they lay against them to sleep.

The wind blew through the unmoving, bleached, dead trees that all streamed in the other direction, beaten thus by the more constant blizzard winds, and all night long the two young horses slept, while the rock sheltered them from the cold that came from the south.

As Baringa started to wake, he was thinking of Benni looking over to the west and saying that there might be some deep and secret places there. So, when he opened his eyes he simply lay there, studying the shadowy land below him.

There did seem to be one very deep, dark cleft. As more light flooded the mountains, he got up and stared down intently.

Now was the time to wander and search, now, when that iron-grey Steel was too stiff and lame to do them any damage.

"We will spend the day in our silver forest," Baringa said to Dawn, "and then, tonight, let us start out to see what is in that deep valley over there. I think we should have a hiding place to which we can go if we need to."

Only the eagles watched them as they played in the silver trees. All day two wedge-tail eagles planed above.

"One would not want them for enemies," said Baringa. "They would know too much."

"You silver horses make friends with all the birds and bush animals, so do not fear," Dawn said.

"Hard to make friends with a wedge-tail -eagle," said Baringa.

In the evening the eagles circled lower and lower with barely a movement of their wings, and landed on the wind-driven branches of one of the dead trees — tremendous dark brown birds with buff markings, enormous curved beaks, strong and cruel, great talons coming out of strong, feathered legs, gripping the branch.

They said nothing, just looked closely at the young horses and took off again.

Baringa reared up to salute the lords of the air, and the eagles dipped their wings and went round them once, seeming to answer his salute.

"They will know he will be a king, such as Thowra," Dawn thought to herself, but she said nothing to Baringa.

As twilight fell — the pale, possum light in which the silver horses became one with their world — Beringa and Dawn went quietly down off The Pilot, westward to a ridge that lay between the Tin Mine Creek and the head of the creek which must run into the cleft that looked so deep and dark at sunset and at dawning.

In the thick timber of the ridge, they found a brumby track, and through the bush on either side flitted the shadows of horses. At last, when darkness enfolded them, it seemed that they, alone, were travellers through the night, except for the bright-eyed possums and a little herd of kangaroos whom they disturbed on a grassy clearing.

After they had gone a long way Baringa turned off the ridge towards the creek, and when he found that the ground became very steep, and he could see nothing in the darkness, he told Dawn they would sleep.

In the morning, at the first piccaninny dawn, he was moving around restlessly, peering down the steep mountainside. This seemed just possible to descend, unlike the sides of Thowra's Secret Valley, for here one could get round the cliffs and scramble down precipitously through trees that seemed to hang on by magic. On the other side of this deep cleft, some of the trees had not hung on, and there were the remains of a great landslide — a long chute of loose stones and a steep slide of bare earth, also a jumble of torn-up trees and logs lying hither and thither.

In a bend of the creek was a high island of perpendicular-sided rock. Its top was capped with trees.

The country looked wild and thrilling.

There was the harsh call of a white-eared honey-eater above them. Baringa jumped, though he knew the little olive-green bird well. He had been so deeply engaged in his own thoughts — imagining that he was galloping for his life, and wondering if this would be a good place to hide — that he was startled by the sudden noise.

The honey-eater went down, down into the depths of the valley.

"We will go too," said Baringa, "and see what we find."

Soon the cliffs and great tree-clad slopes, the wild screes and crags were towering above them. They went farther and farther down where the daylight had not penetrated, rather nervously picking their way, frightened to slide because they would make a noise and set stones rolling, and also because a slide on those dreadful slopes could mean death on rocks over a thousand feet below.

This valley was deeper than the Secret Valley where Baringa was born and bred. He began to wonder if they would get safely down. The air struck cold as they descended, and when he looked up, the climb out looked tremendous.

High above the chasm, the two eagles planed. Baringa felt fairly sure that this time they could not see him, but he took courage from the presence of the lords of the air, and went on.

At the bottom they had to skirt cliffs again, treading carefully, hanging over space, and then they were there, on a green flat enclosed by cliffs.

"This would be a good hiding place," said Baringa, "but we need to find a different way in and out of it."

"We would make a terrible noise if we went down here in a hurry," Dawn said. "Stones rolling, probably us sliding ... but it is indeed a safe place."

They started to walk around, examining everything.

The flat widened and then became a narrow ribbon before the great cliffs closed in completely. Baringa could see no way round these cliffs, nor up them. He slithered down into the stream where the water rushed around his fine legs, tugging at them, pushing. The boulders were rough. It was extremely

difficult to walk. He forced his way along to the point of the
cliff and peered round, but he could only see more cliffs. The
water went through a narrow gorge.

The top end of their flat was also enclosed by cliffs but they
saw that it was possible to climb steeply upwards, over a
jutting-out bluff. Up, up, they went, rock step after rock step.
At last they left the rocks and were in deep forest. The creek
below them was wild and rugged. They went carefully above
it, and soon the valley began opening out.

They saw better country – a string of little grassy places
enclosed by tea tree, and the creek flowing more quietly.
Presently they were on the soft, damp grass and hidden by the
white-starred tea tree.

Baringa went to get a drink from the creek. Suddenly all his
hair pricked up on end. There on the soft, grey sand was a
hoofmark!

He sniffed at it, and he stared and stared. It was almost the
exact shape of Dawn's near forefoot, and Dawn was behind

him and had been behind him all the time, also this spoor was at least an hour old.

He examined the ground all around, but could not see another track. Everywhere else, except just at the creek, there was springy grass in which a horse made no track. They both moved silently up and down the little glade.

It was Dawn who found the silver hair from a mane on a horizontal branch of tea tree.

"How strange," said Baringa. "It is as though you had been here before." And just then he found another hoof-mark, also a near forefoot, and it was broader and stronger — definitely a stallion's.

Dawn looked at it too.

"We had better be careful. That is the print of a stallion older and heavier than you, though perhaps not as fast."

They went on, silently, up the stream. Tea tree grew thickly between each open grass glade, and they pushed their way so gently through it that there was barely the swish of a branch or crack of a twig breaking. At the edge of each glade they waited, hidden in the tea tree, and looked out to make sure there were no other horses. Then they slid out of their cover and explored the glade. Sometimes they found a hoofmark, sometimes some silver hair, and once the hair from a black mane.

Just then a shaft of sunlight pierced the forest and touched the far end of the glade. Baringa jumped — he was so sure he saw, in that shaft of light, a white and silver filly in the tea tree — but then there was nothing. He stayed without moving for a long time, and they did not go out into this glade, just edged around it, always in cover, but they found no further trace of any horse.

They went on up the stream, pushing even more quietly through the tea tree till they came to another, far bigger, open glade. Here they could see some tracks of horses. A small creek came in from one side. Baringa decided to go up that a little way .

This creek was clear all the way up. They had to climb quite sharply on to a broad shelf, and there, at the top end, they could see bones lying.

The two young horses went nervously forward.

"I do not like this place," muttered Baringa. "A horse has died here."

Trembling, they walked forward to look more closely, their feet brushing through the dew, bruising the leaves of a big blue campanula.

"The tail has been silver," muttered Dawn, and Baringa started back nervously.

"Let us go back to the main creek," he said, shivering, and led her down the snowgrass at a trot.

When he had got far enough away to feel more comfortable, he slowed down and stopped to drink.

Dawn said to him:

"There was a grey mare who vanished. I remember her because she had a white and silver filly foal the same age as I, and sired, as I was, by Cloud. I've heard talk of her going and never coming back to Quambat. Those could be her bones, and the track we saw, and the silver hair from a mane, could have been the filly's."

Baringa said nothing. It seemed unbelievable that there could be another filly like Dawn, and yet he felt sure he had seen her.

He led Dawn up the main creek, but they saw no more tracks of the strange filly. As they got nearer the head of the creek, there were signs of more horses, and at last Baringa said:

"The higher parts of this valley will not have a hiding place for us. We must use the canyon we have found. Ahead is a country of many horses," he went on, "and, in the end, if we go over the ridge, there is Quambat Flat and Lightning. Behind us there is a strange stallion whom we did not see, but there is a hiding place. We will go back the way we have come."

Once again Dawn thought, as she followed Baringa, how like Thowra he seemed.

First Snow

Baringa and Dawn stayed away from Quambat for some weeks, but on their own the Canyon was strange and lonely, with its great high walls of mountains towering above and the sunlight only touching the foaming water in the middle of the day, so they roamed farther off where they were never far from other horses.

They grazed around on the ridge-tops and over into the Tin Mine Creek, lower down it than Steel's bimble – but anyway he was still lame – and even into the Ingegoodbee. Many were the times they had to gallop away from other stallions who thought that Dawn should be the beauty of their herd. Baringa had plenty of practice in fighting.

Then one night Baringa remembered Son of Storm, and they visited him and stayed grazing at the trees near him for more days than they could remember. Even if Baringa had many fights with young horses who grazed nearby, he and Dawn were secure in their friendship with Son of Storm.

Son of Storm was just like his father, a kind and noble horse. Though he wondered where Lightning was, he let days go by before he mentioned him, and in those days watched Baringa gallop and play and fight, and realised that often the quick-silver young stallion seemed as though he was imagining his opponent to be a bigger, stronger horse – as though he had an enemy who was always at the back of his mind. It was obvious that Baringa was already faster than horses a year older than himself, and that when he fought he dodged nimbly, as Thowra did. Steel, of course, was an enemy of the silver horses, all the brumbies had heard that, but Son of Storm wondered for whom else Baringa practised his speed and his dodging, leaping, striking? Always in Baringa's mind there must be a picture of someone whom he might one day have to fight.

One evening when Baringa and Dawn had returned after two or three days away, Son of Storm asked him where Lightning grazed.

A plover was crying somewhere down on the banks of the stream, the sky had the green and copper tinge of a dry, frosty autumn evening. Baringa took a little while to answer.

"At the Quambat," he said. "I will return there sometime."

"I see," said Son of Storm slowly. "It is not good for one of the Silver Herd to fight another."

"No," said Baringa shortly. "It is not."

"I see," said Son of Storm again and looked thoughtfully, and perhaps rather sadly, towards Dawn.

Baringa looked at her too, and then asked a question that he felt might almost echo off the copper and green sky:

"Who is the silver filly that hides somewhere in Dale's Creek?"

Silver filly! Silver filly! Perhaps the plovers might cry it, or the ducks winging across the lonely evening sky.

64

"You wander far and wide," said Son of Storm. "Are tales told of a silver filly?"

"No," said Baringa. "I am sure I have seen her!"

"You have *seen* her?" exclaimed Son of Storm.

"Then there are tales told?" Baringa was watching him closely.

"No, not really – or not everywhere – but I have heard tales I never really believed of a silver filly, tales told around that mysterious, wild country that drops deeply towards the Murray. I thought perhaps she was just a dream woven out of the old stories of your grandsire and your dam," Son of Storm looked thoughtful, "and around the same type of country as that which must hide Thowra."

"*I* do not think she is a dream," said Baringa.

"No," the bay replied. "Ever since I saw Dawn I realised that she might, indeed, be real. I searched for her once," he admitted, "before you ever came here, and saw no sign of her, but I know that over there," he tossed his head in the direction of the great, deep valley, "there is a great hole in the hills, a deep-cut valley between steep mountains. I have thought of it several times, for I feel you will not be safe for long – that you are not really safe now. Have you perhaps found it already?"

"I think perhaps I have. Do you know of a way down?"

"No," answered Son of Storm. "I have only looked down and been certain that in such a place must my father's half-brother, Thowra, king of the wind, hide."

Baringa was quiet for a few moments, then he asked:

"What are the tales of the silver filly?"

"Just that she is fabulously beautiful, but never really seen – and that the stallion with whom she runs is exceptionally strong, and also ugly. I do not think *she* could be more beautiful than Dawn."

"It would not be possible to be more beautiful than Dawn," said Baringa.

Occasionally, as the autumn grew sharper and colder, Baringa and Dawn visited their hiding place – till they were sure that in tempest or mist, darkness or blizzard they could put their feet unerringly in each stepping place on the rather hazardous way down.

It was on one of these expeditions that they met Benni and

Silky again. Baringa had wondered a good deal about the kangaroos, but often before they had not seen Benni for a long time, even though the country round the Secret Valley had been his home, so he had not really worried.

This time Baringa and Dawn were going quietly along the ridge above the immense, mysterious cleft in the mountains, when they saw, immobile, as though it were carved out of granite, the form of a kangaroo, sitting, nose to wind, forepaws held in front of his chest.

"It is Benni, it is Benni!" said Baringa.

He knew too much to go hurrying forward, making a noise, so he and Dawn arrived at Benni's side silently, though of course Benni, with the age-old eyes of the Australian bush, had seen them.

Even Dawn shyly extended her lovely nose for the kangaroo's soft pat, and Baringa gently lipped the pointed grey ears.

"Well," said Benni. "We called in at Quambat Flat and saw only Lightning. He could not – or would not – tell us anything about you, but the mare, Cirrus, who says she belongs to the Silver Stallion, told us that she was certain you were all right, and that Cloud had given Steel a fearful beating. However, we saw Steel, who is recovered, and we have reason to believe he is more dangerous to you silver horses than ever. Where have you been?"

"We have been wandering a lot, but if we are anywhere for any length of time," said Baringa, "it is either down in our canyon or with Son of Storm."

"Ah," said Benni. "You have found a hiding place, and you went to Son of Storm." He looked at Baringa with the same expression of respect as that with which Thowra had looked at him when the yearling had tracked him. Also this beautiful, fiery, young colt still had with him the loveliest filly that Benni had seen in the mountains.

"You have indeed received the qualities which Bel Bel gave to Thowra," said Silky's voice.

Baringa jumped. He had not seen Silky. However clever a wild horse made himself, the animals and the birds of the bush had belonged to the land for thousands of years, and they could make themselves absolutely invisible, and their eyes could see what a horse's eye would never see.

"Come," said Benni. "Let us go down into your mysterious canyon. In all our wandering through the south we have found

66

no place that we liked better than The Pilot – and it would be a little exposed in bad weather."

"Good," said Baringa. "Perhaps you may make our canyon your home – but it won't get much sun in winter."

The kangaroos hopped along after the silver colt and his silver filly, followed them, as night fell, steeply down into the dark depths, over rocky cliffs, down stony places where the trees clung to slopes so precipitous that they could barely stay on them themselves. Then they went down behind the rock bluff and at last they were on the floor of the Canyon, beside rushing water.

"It is a grand hiding place," said Baringa, "but it is not as near to Quambat as I would have liked."

"Can't have everything," said Benni. "I suppose you wanted to have a hiding place there so that it would seem as if the ground opened to hide you whenever Lightning tried to steal your filly!"

A gleam of amusement lit Baringa's eyes even in the darkness.

"It might be possible," said Benni, "to reach this place more quickly from Quambat if you could find a way down from the other side."

"Have to slide down a scree – so far down," Baringa answered, but he was thinking that he had never been on that high plateau on the other side, the plateau that ended the Quambat Ridge.

The night was steely cold and he felt restless, even lying beside Dawn. He kept thinking that before day broke they should be trying to get on to that plateau and then follow it back towards Quambat. He would quite like to see, from the fringe of the trees, what Lightning was doing. He wondered if they would see any sign of the other silver filly. He wondered when it would snow. He wondered what Thowra and Kunama were doing in the Secret Valley.

Benni refused to leave the Canyon until he had a day exploring it. When daylight came Baringa realised this was wisest!

"You have the restlessness that comes before snow falls," Benni said.

All day they examined the opposite walls of the Canyon, searched for a crossing place of the creek that would be safe even in spring. The opposite side offered nothing but unrelenting cliffs except at one place where, if they could get across to it, there looked to be several interconnecting shelves zig-zagging up the cliff.

"You and Dawn would look like white butterflies flying down the face of that cliff," Benni said cheerfully. "It is, however, a good kangaroo track."

Baringa gave him a playful nudge with his nose.

"Very wet at the bottom," he teased, but the fever of restlessness – snow fever – was urging him on. He forced a crossing of the creek on to a tiny shingle beach, scrambled precariously up the first few feet of cliff and then found himself on a shelf that led upwards.

Twilight was gathering in the floor of the Canyon. There would be no bright light to shine on their coats. Baringa waited for Dawn. She crossed the cold stream and joined him on his shelf.

"Benni says that Silky is tired," she said. "They will see us tonigl : – or tomorrow."

"Benni does not like cold water," Baringa was amused.

He led the way up each zig-zag shelf. The shelves did not actually go up so very steeply, but the cliff, itself, the great leaping side of the mountain, was almost straight up and down. To the kangaroos, below, the two silver horses did indeed look like moths alighted on the rock wall, and then fluttering upwards.

Each time Baringa looked down, he was afraid and yet wildly excited by being right out in space above the immense drop into the darkening valley. The filly followed him serenely.

They were sweating before they were half-way up, and the air slid over their hot coats with chill touch.

Baringa carefully noted each step they took on each shelf. Perhaps they would come back in darkness. Perhaps . . . someday . . . perhaps they might come down it, escaping. Each step took them closer to the lighter sky, and yet the night rose up and up beneath them, hiding the great, deep Canyon.

A wind had started to blow.

They pulled themselves off the last shelf over the edge on to the ridge-top. Night engulfed them. Trees blew in the dark wind, stretching wild arms to the wild sky. Then down – cold on nose, back and rump – fell the first flakes of snow.

"Quick," said Baringa. "We must go a little way along this

68

high ridge before we go back." Through the spattering snow and the windy dark he could see the eager gleam in Dawn's eyes.

Together they went on through the wind and the snow and the night.

Trees blew hither and thither, changing shapes with each rush of wind. Baringa knew it would be almost impossible to recognise the country again when they returned for home, yet they pressed on eagerly as though there was a secret retreating from them. Each cold touch of the snow on face, on trembling ears, only added to his excitement.

His heart gave an enormous jolt within him when he came on the first trace of other horses. He and Dawn searched all around, but the falling snow, the wild-blowing wind, made it impossible to see the strand of silver mane or tail which Baringa half expected to find.

Once he shot forward through the trees because he was certain that, ahead, he saw a gleam of light or falling snow or silver hide, the shape of beauty flitting through the wind-tossed trees. He looked back, and there was the shape of beauty behind him, as Dawn cantered lightly through the snow.

They went on, but they saw no other wisp of moving white except the falling snow, as it beat harder and harder in their faces. At last Baringa stopped. He wondered whether to stay where they were for the rest of the snowy night, or to go back to the Canyon before their way was completely transformed by snow.

He looked around. The forest had been moving so constantly in the wind and the weaving snow that he knew he would not recognise anything, that only his sense of direction would take them back.

Dawn was dancing and leaping in the wind-whirling snow. He followed her round and round, rearing and cavorting, dancing to winter and to the falling snow — and yet dancing to drive away the eerie aloneness of that great, high plateau where the dark trees waved twisted limbs to the dark sky.

Then they both dropped on to their feet and started trotting purposefully in the direction of the Canyon, back to the friendly company of the kangaroos. And the wind-whirled world changed around them all the time, the snow hid stone and log, hid every landmark.

69

Unerringly Baringa led through this constantly moving world. He could see no shape he knew, but ahead there was something drawing him. This was the way, he was certain, and he went on, on, into the biting wind – this way, this way only – something drew him on with the snow beating on eyes, on nose, on forehead, drawing him on, right to the edge of the cliff and the first shelf that led down into the Canyon.

Then, through the wind and the beating snow, hidden from everyone, the two white horses walked down the shelves on the cliff face towards their canyon, leaving behind them the high, lonely plateau.

Baringa took with him the memory of an illusive wisp of white hide or hair that perhaps might only have been the falling snow, and the haunting impression of an eerie land.

An Unbelievable Chase

Not much snow fell, but it kept on falling for several days.

Down in the Canyon with Dawn and the kangaroos, Baringa was still restless. He was thinking of the strange land up above, he was wondering what Lightning was doing at Quambat Flat. He could not help wishing that he, himself, could be safe in the Secret Valley with Thowra, before winter came.

Perhaps Benni understood all this, for he said, on the evening of the second day:

"I think we should go out of the Canyon and head towards the Gap where Storm and the herd run. Now that snow is falling, Thowra may come out to see you and Lightning. He said he would come before the winter – and the winter is here."

"Let us go, then," said Baringa. "Come on!" And he started straight off for the way out of the Canyon towards the Tin Mine Creek.

"Impatient," said Benni, shaking his head. "Wild horses are always impatient!" But Benni and Silky knew they were glad to be on the move too. When winter really came, then one needed to be safely and comfortably settled in a place with plenty of food, but just now, when the first snow was falling, was a strange, restless time. It was good to be hopping along through the snowy bush, following the trotting horses.

70

At Quambat Flat the light snow fell and barely lay on the ground. The wind howled up above in the Cobras. Goonda shivered and began to think of the herd she had left on the Gap below Stockwhip Hill. Lightning roamed around without ceasing. *He* had no great love for the Secret Valley and did not wish to return there, but he wished Baringa were with him at Quambat. He would almost leave him in peace with Dawn if he could have the comfort of his company.

It would have been fun to gallop and play together in the cold and snow-filled air.

Only a few flakes fell in the Secret Valley.

Thowra saw a robin redbreast flying through a curtain of snow, and he went up the cliff path again, joyously, joyously out to the mountains.

The wombat that lived in the cliff peered out of his hole as the Silver Brumby went upwards with springy, eager step.

"The mountains will be woken up for a while before the heavy snow falls," he thought, and he wondered where the two young colts had gone when they went southwards, away from the men, the roads, and the machines of which all the bush animals had heard by now. "Three silver stallions," he thought, "running in the southern mountains!"

Thowra went towards the Crackenback first, to see what was going on there, and looked with uncomprehending eyes at the wide road above the river where he had once had such trouble to cross his mares and foals in springtime. Then he hurried on for the Cascades, trotting, trotting through the falling snow.

There were a few horses in the Cascades. Thowra felt their presence, and smelt them, but did not see them. It did cross his mind that Storm might have returned to his beloved country, so he called aloud once and then again, and his great cry rang around the Cascades as it had rung years ago, but there was no answer. Storm must still be grazing on the Gap where he had left him.

The snow fell more thickly as the night darkened. The great Silver Stallion went on alone, southward through the driving storm, and the needle-cold snow stung his eyes, his ears, his nostrils, fell on his withers, his back, flanks, rump, each sharp needle transmitting an electric shock — a shock of wild excitement. Snow on the tussocks of snowgrass brushed against his fetlocks, cold, thrilling cold. Snow began to cling to his coat. As he neared the Gap he heard the wind cry in the high rock tors. He flung up his head to neigh, but stopped. It might be more fun to be silent, to go through the shrouding snow, unseen and unheard, till the time came to say: "It is I, Thowra!"

It was not Storm on whom he wished to creep unawares. There was a certain white-faced, blue stallion. . . .

Thowra broke into a dancing, light-footed canter. Life was very good. Just now, while the first snows of winter were falling, he would claim his mountain kingdom. . . . He would also have a look to see where his son and grandson were, and how they were going to live during the winter.

The wind howled through the Gap: the snow whirled, swirled. Thowra rose in a half-rear, listening, feeling, then shook the snow from his forelock and mane, and went purposefully and quietly down towards the valley where he had first seen old Whiteface.

It took him a little while to get down, because he wanted to be sure that he made no faintest sound, and that his movements were so slow that no one could distinguish him from the moving snow.

He was in the valley.

With infinite slowness he went forward.

Whiteface stood sound asleep, barked into the trees on the windward side of the valley.

Slowly, slowly Thowra flowed through the snow and the wind and the night till he was beside him. Then he blew out through his nose, without much sound, into the ear of the sleeping horse.

A long shiver went through Whiteface.

"It is the wind," Thowra whispered.

Whiteface jumped as if his ear had been bitten again, and swung around. His sleeping eyes flew open and he looked feverishly about him.

"Oh, it's you, is it?" he said, trying to change his angry tone to one of politeness, for he had no wish to get another beating.

"What news?" asked Thowra.

"It snows, and winter comes," replied Whiteface.

"I *knew* Suggan Buggan was the place for you!" Thowra bit him swiftly on one ear. "*Now* tell me!"

"Steel, son of The Brolga, is coming this way for some reason that I do not know. The birds of the air tell that he has visited Quambat and sworn death to all silver horses," Whiteface answered hurriedly.

"That's interesting," said Thowra. "Perhaps he will teach my son and grandson to fight. Coming this way, you say? Maybe I shall meet him. You may go on with your wondrous deep sleep. I will see you again," and he vanished into the snow and the night.

Whiteface shook himself. He had been frightened. He was angry. He was glad to be alive. He wandered around looking at his herd to make sure that no one had followed the ghostly will o' the wisp through the snow – or to make sure that he had really gone. Only Lightning had taken any of the mares or fillies with him, the first time that the silver horse had come, but Whiteface knew that the lovely, pale strawberry roan mare would follow Thowra to the last mountain rampart if Thowra so much as called once.

However Thowra had neither stayed nor called.

Thowra had found Storm and then gone on, down the brumby track towards the Tin Mines, seeking Steel.

Further down, out of the wind, the snow was falling in big flakes, straight down, softly, softly. No longer did wind-driven pellets sting eyes and ears. Thowra followed the track down and down.

At last he was among the mountain ash. The tall trees were hidden in darkness and the close-falling flakes, but he knew where he was by the sighing of the bark streamers, the whispering silence, the sharp and lovely scent.

Then it happened! There, in the murmuring forest, Thowra was spellbound by magic like his own.

Suddenly he knew that, in that whispering silence, there were others around him, invisible and noiseless, as he himself was invisible and noiseless – others close among the great tall trunks, other ghosts moving, other ghosts breathing.

Thowra stood absolutely still, hardly breathing himself.

He was sure that whoever they were came closer and closer. Surely the hop-scrub around his legs moved slightly!

A sudden flurry of snow blinded him – and a soft paw patted him on the nose!

There was the smell of kangaroo.

"Benni!" he whispered, bowing his head to the kangaroo's

– and then he saw, through the great, drifting flakes, the faint suggestion of two statue horses.

He stood quite still, staring, though the snow coated his eyelashes.

It was Baringa, grown bigger, stronger. It was not Lightning beside him. Who was it? Who? Who? For Thowra saw a white and silver filly of exquisite beauty. It was Dawn grown up, grown more lovely.

Baringa had inherited something from his grandsire, Thowra thought, for that filly was glorious – and he still had her with him!

Thowra and Baringa both rose in the half-rear of greeting and, as they rose, a sound broke the stillness, the challenging neigh of a stallion, not very far distant.

Thowra dropped on to his four feet and said softly:

"Steel?"

"Yes, Steel," Baringa answered. "He would kill us all, if he could."

"Well, he can't," said Thowra, "but now I understand why he comes this way."

"He would even kill your yearling grandson," Benni said, and Thowra could tell that his lip was curling. "He tried to kill Lightning, but Baringa drew him away. He fights the young ones who cannot hurt him – which other stallions never do – but he hates and fears the presence of silver horses."

"Perhaps," said Thowra, "I had better kill him – but killing I have never enjoyed. Anyway," and he gave Baringa a playful nip, "you must grow in strength and speed and cunning so that you can protect yourself . . . and your mare," and he looked admiringly from Baringa to Dawn. When he turned back to Baringa there was the same expression of respect in his face as had been there once before.

Benni was sitting at his feet and Thowra nuzzled his ear gently.

"What do you think, Benni?" he asked. "Why should I kill this horse when I want to enjoy myself?"

"I do not know," Benni replied. "He is a bad horse."

"Where is Lightning?" Thowra asked suddenly.

"At Quambat," Baringa replied.

Thowra was thinking of Steel. Years ago he had killed the chestnut Arrow in order that he himself might live. Spear, Arrow's nephew, he had killed so that Kunama would not be

74

captured by him. Now there was Steel, son of The Brolga, whom he had beaten but left alive.

Steel needed a lesson.

"I shall go to find Steel," Thowra said. "You and your filly, Baringa, will follow slowly. And what of you and Silky, O Benni?"

"We will return slowly, too, because we will winter somewhere over there."

So Thowra set off again into the snow and the night.

Before the first daylight crept over the sky he knew he was getting close to Steel, that Steel was coming towards him.

Thowra stopped and waited. The grey stallion showed up very faintly. Thowra waited till he was quite close, then suddenly sprang towards him, roaring with rage.

Steel propped in his tracks. Horrified, he saw the ghostly shape of a huge silver stallion hurtling himself through the air, then he turned and galloped in terror, back the way he had come, Thowra leaping and bounding after him.

Pale light began to creep into the sky and filter downwards through falling snow as Thowra chased Steel along the flat open valleys that led towards the Tin Mines. Occasionally he leapt forward and struck him; often he bit at his fleeing rump.

Other horses peered out of the shelter of snowgums and candlebarks to see who went past through the snow and the dawning. At first they could only see dim shapes galloping, but, as the light grew stronger, the watchers saw the grey only just ahead of the great Silver Stallion, and they could tell that the silver horse was driving him, that any moment, if he wished, he could race in front of the grey horse and force him to stand and fight. Thowra was simply chasing Steel — and enjoying every moment of it.

A whisper went through the bush, from horse to horse, from possum to wombat. The first kurrawongs cried it to the wild sky.

"It is Thowra! The silver horse is here!"

Son of Storm, standing beneath a big candlebark saw the two horses, Thowra with stores of energy still unused, and Steel showing signs of exhaustion. He saw them racing up the valley, heard the snap of Thowra's teeth.

Son of Storm decided to follow and see what happened, for he knew well that Steel intended to kill both Baringa and Lightning. Also, this was something he had never seen nor heard of — one stallion chasing and driving another, wildly, madly, along the open valleys.

As Steel began to flag, Thowra paused for a moment and then leapt on to a rock and cried his wild joy through the snow-filled air — through the bush, while all other creatures watched, waited and listened.

"It is Thowra!" they whispered, and every animal and bird knew he was strong, fast, joyous, beautiful and wise, so that he owned his world.

The sweat streamed faster down Steel's coat as he heard Thowra's ringing cry. Then Thowra was after him again turning him up into the bush on the ridge which divided the Ingegoodbee from the Tin Mine Creek, driving him back to his own bimble.

Son of Storm followed and, as Storm went stumbling out of the bush into the valley, he hid himself at the edge of the timber, where he could see what happened.

When Thowra had forced Steel out into the open, snowy valley, he galloped round and stood in front of him, and just then, in a shaft that illuminated the falling snow, sunlight came through the clouds to fall direct on Thowra, shining on him magnificently.

76

Thowra raised one foreleg as though to strike.

"By such as you, my son and grandson will not be molested," he said. "Remember! Or I will return again and assuredly kill you. Now I call on all the animals of the bush and the birds of the air to witness this. Until Lightning and Baringa are of an age to protect themselves, you shall not harm them."

There was a cry of kurrawongs above, and through the snow came the beat of eagles' wings and the shadow of them passed over Thowra. Then out of the bush stepped Son of Storm.

"I, too, will bear witness," he said, and went up to Thowra, standing beside the great silver horse in his shaft of sunlight, as Storm had often stood beside him.

The sunlight faded and the snow swirled around them.

Thowra, in company with Son of Storm, grazed near Steel for an hour or so, keeping the grey constantly breaking out into a sweat of fear.

All through that time, while the falling snow clothed the land, the brumbies of the country round the Tin Mines crept up through the fringe of forest and looked at the immense silver horse grazing in the open country; the birds of the air flew past to look: a few inquiring kangaroos bounded in their ancient rhythm through the trees, everyone looking at the glorious horse of whom they had heard.

Then Baringa, with Dawn, Benni and Silky, came silently out of the bush, and the silence in the forest and the wide valley was intense, for there were the loveliest horses that had ever been seen, the stallion, the young colt, and the dream-like filly.

And one brumby might say to another:

"They are the horses of the Silver Herd, but is it she? Is it she of whom the birds tell?"

Only the birds could have whispered:

"Not she, not the Hidden One, but one as lovely."

Thowra was wondering about something. As they grazed he asked Baringa where he usually ran.

"Sometimes with Son of Storm, sometimes above the Tin Mine Creek . . . sometimes in a hidden place. . . . Sometimes I go to The Pilot," he replied.

Thowra said nothing. An hour or so later he touched noses with Son of Storm and set off towards the Quambat.

Baringa's ears flickered forward and flickered back. He looked at Dawn, walking beside him.

If Thowra noticed his uneasiness, he made no sign, just continued towards the south.

They still had three or four miles to go when Baringa said to Thowra:

"It is not for me, yet, to take Dawn back to Quambat. We will turn west here, and perhaps see you as you go back."

Thowra stopped and looked at Baringa.

"I wish you to come," he said. "While I am with you – and after I have gone – nothing will befall Dawn or you." Then he went onwards more swiftly, so that Baringa could say nothing.

The young colt kept looking at Dawn and back to his silver grandsire.

There was Lightning waiting at Quambat. "We are Thowra's grandson and son," he thought, and the son was the elder, the stronger, the one of an age to be gathering his own herd. Baringa wondered, but he could only put his trust in Thowra, the king.

Through the drifting snow came the cry of a kurrawong, and once Baringa heard the strange raucous call of the wedge-tail eagles – the king of the birds, and the king of the wild horses – but somehow the eagles had seemed to be taking an interest in *him*.

It was growing dusk, and the snow still falling, when they reached the top of Quambat Flat. Quiet, quiet fell the snow through the grey-green eucalypt leaves, down grey-brown bark, down the white smoothness of candlebarks. Quiet were their footsteps in the snow, and each hoofmark, uncovering grass, was soon filled in by the heavier falling flakes. Cold fell the flakes on silver hide and the grey fur of the kangaroos.

Baringa felt a thrill of excitement and apprehension flash and tingle through him. Here he was at Quambat again with Dawn! He knew he was fast and nimble, but he was still not strong enough to beat a horse one whole year older than himself – and Dawn was so beautiful.

Cloud and Mist were out in the open, a little way down the flat. Cirrus was grazing near the trees only a few yards from the soft-footed silver horses. Thowra went nearer to her, as silent as a zephyr of air, but, in every line of his body, the pent-up energy of the whirlwind.

From the trees beside her he sent the whisper of a neigh through his nostrils.

"It is I, the wind!"

Cirrus raised her lovely, calm head, and moved towards him. Then they walked together to greet the two grazing greys.

"Hail, O Cloud," said Thowra walking forward ceremoniously. "I have returned, as I said I would, and I thank you for the safety you have given my son and grandson."

"Hail, O Silver Stallion," Cloud replied. "Welcome to the Quambat. Your son grazed further down the flat, as for Baringa," and he looked at the silver colt behind Thowra with that same gleam of respect in his eyes, "he has managed his own affairs — and my daughter's — with courage and wisdom."

"I thank you for your kind words," Thowra inclined his head. "But I have brought Baringa back to you for the winter — that he and your daughter may graze safely with you until the spring."

"Indeed, that they may do, and for longer," Cloud replied.

"By this spring," Thowra said, and he spoke as much to the young colt as to Cloud. "Baringa will be old enough to hold mares of his own, though to hold one as beautiful as Dawn will be hard for a two-year-old."

"He, little more than a yearling, has done it so far," Cloud said.

"I go now to see Lightning," Thowra announced. "Baringa and Dawn I will leave with you." He touched Baringa's nose, looked at Dawn once with puzzled admiration, and he and Cirrus walked away together through the curtain of falling snow.

Cirrus returned the next morning, but Thowra had gone in the snow and the wind.

Echo in the Ice-cold Night

Dawn, of course, knew that there was a magnificence about Baringa, a suggestion of fiery glory, and while Thowra was there she had a strong feeling that both Thowra and Cloud realised there was this quality in the silver colt.

She knew in every bone, in every vein, in every white and silver hair of her hide, that Baringa had this quality which Lightning had not — but Lightning was strong and a whole year older than Baringa. Dawn could not help fearing that, in spite of Thowra, in spite of Cloud, he might hurt the younger and most beautiful horse — hurt him because of *her* — for she had seen quite clearly that Lightning wanted her for his herd.

However, winter had come, and the snow, and in the time of snow food-finding became most important for animals who live in the wild bush. No one thinks of much else — except perhaps, just sometimes, the young and the gay. Also Thowra had spoken. . . .

Baringa himself knew that even Thowra's command could not stop Lightning's jealousy. He would rather not have come to Quambat — yet, even when they were with Benni, or visiting Son of Storm, the bush was lonely in the snow, and the wind, and the rain of winter. Lightning was brother to Baringa's own dam, Cloud was the sire of Dawn, Cirrus was now owned by Thowra: here, at Quambat, the place which Thowra had chosen for them, it was as though they were part of his own herd — but for this winter he and Dawn must live their lives with great care.

However much Baringa wanted to see Lightning, to romp with him in the cold air, he could not help wondering if Lightning might not try to steal Dawn.

Lightning had followed Cirrus, after Thowra had gone, but he did not come far up the flat.

Baringa saw him.

He murmured to Dawn to wait, and went walking down through the snow to greet him. He held his head high, as though with pride, but he felt immensely alone.

Lightning, after one swift glance to see where Dawn was, greeted him with pleasure, and they reared, and bucked, and danced around each other, quite excited to be together again, even if the thought of Dawn were at the back of each of their minds. They played, but they were both hungry, and soon they started scratching under the snow for the poor grass.

Baringa steadily grazed his way back to Dawn, and though Lightning came closer, he made no sign that he was interested in her.

They were very hungry.

It stopped snowing that evening and became far colder. Baringa and Dawn huddled together for warmth beneath a snowgum and were glad when Cirrus came under their tree too. The next day was bright and sunny, but so cold that the snow barely melted. Only the icy wind blew it. At night stars glittered in the great, cold sky, and feathery frost formed on the surface of the snow, on leaves, on stems of grass or thistles, on the eyelashes of a horse, on the soft fur of a kangaroo.

The young horses played in the frost, next morning, pawing at the dancing prisms, tossing the crystals up towards the sun, but the older ones started the serious business of searching for food immediately it was light. As the sun went down in the clear, greeny sky, and the cold clamped down again, the horses were all still hungry.

In the days that followed, the sun slightly softened the snow, and then the bitter frost at night turned it all into solid ice. The two little creeks that meet on Quambat Flat, and are the start of the Murray River, were ribbons of ice.

Even Cloud and Mist moved from their usual grazing ground at the top end of the flat, hoping to find grass or shrubs to eat, and the young horses went with them, returning as dark fell.

Baringa and Dawn were both nervous. They had never felt hungry like this before, and the hungrier they got, the colder they felt at night. Then one evening, as the bitter cold pressed down on them, Benni and Silky came hopping in under the shelter of their tree, and there was comfort in the presence of the soft kangaroos.

"Do not be afraid," Benni said. "This will be a hard winter, but we will live through it," and later, when even the kindly Cirrus was asleep, he whispered to Baringa that they might try his Secret Canyon, and see if, there, the depth of the valley and the height of the sheltering cliffs had preserved the grass at all from the frost and the ice.

81

In the morning Baringa and Dawn and the kangaroos went down to the lower end of the flat with the other horses, but Baringa and Benni had planned to move quietly away through the trees when Lightning was not looking.

Lightning and Goonda were down there already. In the cold weather Goonda had become darker, as the red hair thickened in her coat. She was quiet and nervous, and very hungry, as were all the mares who were in foal or with a foal at foot. She was becoming quite a pretty mare. Lightning rarely left her side, but on this morning, as soon as he realised that Baringa and Dawn and the kangaroos had gone, he slipped away himself, trying to track them through the icy snow.

For once Lightning was clever – or lucky – for he caught a glimpse of Dawn's coat through the trees. Perhaps he had looked in the right direction because he had heard the rumours that were whispered around among the horses that somewhere to the north of Quambat there had once been seen a most beautiful filly – white and silver. Since no horse had seen more than the vanishing image of her, she was whispered to be wild and lovely as a dream.

Lightning went quickly, once he was hidden in the trees, but when he reached the place where he had seen Dawn, she was gone, and only the memory of a vanished, lovely filly was there.

He tried to find their tracks. Here and there he thought the ice was marked, but it was as though the young horses could run without touching the snow, for he really found no tracks at all.

Then he saw Dawn's flowing tail, far ahead – or did he imagine it? Did he really see something silver in the bush, there and then gone?

For a long time he kept thinking there was the movement of a silver colt or filly. He trotted on and on, sometimes sliding on the icy snow, sometimes breaking through. Sometimes snow, frozen on to a branch, whipped his flanks.

Then he began to feel the silent loneliness of the bush close in around him. He had seen no wombats, nor kangaroos nor wallabies; even the birds were quiet in the intense cold as they carried on their search for food. Once he saw two wedge-tail eagles, high above, and did not know that the king of the birds watched over Baringa.

Lightning stopped, stood still and wondered. It was then

that he saw Baringa and Dawn, for sure, some distance away, crossing a glade.

He sprang after them — and his hooves slid on the ice, rattled on a dead log. The noise he made carried to the listening ears of the kangaroos as well as the silver colt and his silver filly.

Baringa propped, sniffed the wind, flickered his ears.

"Lightning!" he said, and he changed his direction from almost due north to east, on to what was quite a well-used brumby track. He took care that Lightning should see him and hear him quite often, and he began to travel rather faster.

"We will lead him on to the Tin Mine Track," Baringa whispered to Benni. "Then we will let him pass and go back."

Dawn shivered. What if Lightning had become cleverer and found them?

They reached the track and Baringa noticed that horses had been along it both ways. He jumped lightly across it, and all four of them hid themselves in the bush fairly close. Presently they could hear Lightning coming.

Dawn felt herself shivering uncontrollably with fear. Lightning must *not* find them now. A leaf touched her back and she almost jumped. Baringa, she saw, was calm, unworried. Then Lightning came into sight. She stood tensely still.

She watched Lightning turn rather slowly towards the Tin Mine ("He's remembering Steel," she thought) and go round a bend in the track.

A little time passed before Baringa moved, then he slid quietly through the bushes, jumped the track, and cut across through the pathless bush towards the head of the creek that flowed through his Secret Canyon — the creek on whose bank he had first seen the hoofmark and strand of silver hair.

The little springs and bogs at the head of the creek were all frozen. The sphagnum swamps were hidden under the icy snow. The soft warm country seemed completely altered. Baringa wondered where that hidden silver filly had spent the winter, but all the time he was wondering this, half his mind was thinking that Lightning could not have seen them go but must have known in which direction they were likely to head.

Baringa moved along faster. Probably Lightning would turn for home soon: anyway it was most unlikely that he would come seeking and exploring all on his own, with the world frozen like this.

This valley, even covered in frozen snow, would be better

winter quarters than that high, wild plateau between the Canyon and the Murray. Baringa, as he thought of this, went even more carefully. Somehow he felt sure that, even if he might never catch more than a flashing glimpse of the silver filly, the ugly stallion would assuredly show himself, and fight, and who was he, Baringa, to think of winning the Hidden Filly? Far more likely that her ugly stallion would beat him and take Dawn.

Though he was cold and hungry, Baringa felt a flame creeping through him. It was good to be alive: it was good to be here, in this valley of the mysterious silver filly – country that he might one day make his own, and a strange, shy silver mare that he might sometime fight for and claim. Baringa was excited, every sense alert, ears pricked, every hair tingling.

He led his little party on and on, through the tangle of bush down the valley. Then suddenly he found softened snow and two sets of hoofprints – those which were exactly similar to Dawn's, and the broad, strong, heavy mark of the stallion.

His blood raced. He looked all around. Except on that one soft patch there were no tracks. Dawn searched too. She was curious about her half-sister whom no one ever saw, whose hoofmarks were the exact counterpart of her own, whose hair was silver, the same as hers.

A tangle of tea-tree scrub grew in a dense band across the creek. Snow had melted on its leaves and twigs, and then frozen again into prisms of ice, catching and reflecting the light from a thousand different facets. The glitter of it shone in Baringa's eyes, making him blink. Then he peered through his eyelashes, trying to see beyond the glitter and fire of light, because surely, oh surely, *she* was hidden there. But he could see nothing.

With the little hanging prisms of ice and the ice-coated leaves touching him, sharp, cold, Baringa crept through the tea tree. There was nothing, nothing.

All day long, right up until they came to the canyon cliffs, Baringa kept expecting to see the flowing mane or tail, but they saw no one, and they dropped down into the Canyon, *his* Secret Valley, late in the afternoon.

There was not so much snow in the Canyon and here and there, in little sheltered pockets they found some grass that had not been too badly spoilt by the frost.

Benni, Silky, Baringa, Dawn – they put their heads down and ate. When darkness fell they slept beneath a candlebark and an overhang of rock, and were warmer and less hungry than they had been since the frosts started. They were warm and comfortable, but they were a long way from other horses. All night long the creek went past, quietly, quietly, stilled by frost. All night long the bitter-bright stars moved across their arc of sky.

Baringa knew that they could hardly have stayed there without Benni and Silky; they would have felt too much alone. Even now it was only the thought of the good grass that stopped him saying:

"Come. Let us go back!"

In the morning, the world seemed different! They grazed happily, and really began to feel full, and by nightfall the Canyon was theirs again, not strange nor hostile as it had been the night before. They slept soundly.

Day broke with red streamers of cloud high in the sky.

"Wind," said Baringa, and Benni gave him a playful tap on the nose.

"Becoming wise, aren't you?" he teased, and added firmly: "We are in the right place to be protected from bad wind," for he knew that Baringa would get wild and restless when the wind blew, and perhaps afraid of being away from older horses.

"Yes," said Baringa doubtfully, but Benni knew so much more than he did.

"Here the grass is still good," said Benni, trying to make himself feel sure.

"Yes," said Baringa, starting to graze.

They did not notice the first eddies of wind, deep down there in the Canyon. Once when Benni saw Baringa looking upwards he said:

"The wind will roar across the Quambat tonight, and you will sleep here quietly in your canyon. The wind will roar up above, but here will be quiet." Benni was still trying to persuade himself as much as Baringa, and had no thought that he might be wrong.

The first thing that disturbed them was not the storm, but a wild, echoing neigh.

It was impossible to tell where the cry came from. It seemed to drop into the Canyon and then ring from one wall to the other, back and forth.

85

Baringa nearly neighed with fright himself, and even Benni jumped.

"Some horse must be coming down into the Canyon," said Baringa, when the echoes had ceased. Before Benni could reply, the neigh rang out again.

"I don't think so," Benni said at last. "I think it is a trick of the wind, but I'll go and see while you look after Silky and Dawn."

"But I must come," said Baringa.

"No," Benni replied sharply. "If The Ugly One, by any chance, should see you in here, it would be very bad. There were no signs of horses ever having been in this canyon. If you want it to be yours, he must never come here, so stay hidden!" Benni did not wait for any further argument, but hopped off, half hidden in the bush that grew along the cliffs.

Benni was puzzled. He really wondered if the ugly stallion was near the cliff at the head of the Canyon, but even there, and along the steep, rough hillside above the creek, they had seen no signs of horses.

As he hopped on quietly the neigh came again. There was something very queer about the way it echoed. Now he was certain it did not come from the top of the Canyon.

"Bamboozled!" he said to himself. "I will stand and listen." Then, when he listened, he thought it came from the cliffs above. "It must come on the wind," he murmured, and turned down the Canyon again. After a few hops he started to peer up at that high, wild plateau at the end of the Qumbat Ridge. If a horse was there he would barely be able to see him, but now each time he heard the sound he was sure that was where it came from. Benni stood like a small grey shadow of centuries past, paws folded in front, and he listened.

There it was, the echoing, weird neigh, dropping down, circling round him, and then again, coming in a different way, crying straight up the Canyon. He shivered.

If it was The Ugly One, and he was sure it was, his close-ness was a danger to Baringa, perhaps more of a danger than the closeness of Steel would be.

Benni could not see anything that looked like the shape of a horse anywhere above. There was no movement on the cliffs, no silhouette against the sky. Up on the edge of the plateau only the trees moved in the wind. Before he went back to the others he went right up to the cliff at the top of the flat, just to assure himself that the neigh did not come from there and echo. But there was no horse to be seen, and the sound did not start from there. He hopped slowly and thoughtfully back through the scrub. These silver horses were certainly a responsiblity!

"Baringa!" he said sharply, when he had told all he had to tell. "Do not look like that!"

"Like what?" asked Baringa.

"Well, up to no good," Benni answered. "Do not try to find them. Tonight there will be bad wind."

"Tonight I stay here in the warmth of our overhanging rock, the quietness of the Canyon," Baringa answered. "Tomorrow I may go exploring – and don't fear that your paws will freeze in the stream, O Benni, for it is not necessary to accompany me!"

Benni boxed his nose ... Then they all stood listening to the echoing neigh.

By now they could also hear the wind talking in the trees high above them. The unquiet night began to close down, and then, through the icy gloom, there came a moaning sound up the Canyon, sometimes a wail.

"It is the wind," said Benni.

"What!" mocked Baringa, though his coat was staring with fear (for horses are so akin to the wind that it stirs them deeply). "What! Were you wrong, O Benni? Is our canyon going to be as filled with the noise of the wind as the Quambat?"

"It seems that I shall have to admit that I was wrong," Benni replied with dignity, at which Baringa gently nipped one little pointed ear.

"Provided you stop biting me," said Benni, shaking his head, "it will not be such a rough night here as it will be at Quambat, but the wind is now blowing straight up the gorge. Even these trees are tossing."

"We will be more comfortable here – or less uncomfortable," said Silky suddenly, "and we are full of quite good grass."

"Yes," said Benni. "Let us get under our rock and sleep."

The two young horses were very restless, for the wind would not let them be still. All night long there was the sound of it wailing between the narrow rocks. All night long Baringa stirred and stirred, even listening through sleep for that neigh to be borne into the Canyon. For Baringa knew that, provided he did not have Dawn with him, he was not really afraid of

87

The Ugly One. Every day Baringa grew older, and stronger – and *faster*.

The wind raged over the mountains through the darkness, and when the first glimmer of dawn broke, wildly travelling clouds covered the sky. Baringa was ready to go ... because he knew he must.

He had told Dawn, during the night, that she must stay with Benni.

"I swear that unless anything happens to me, someday your sister will run with you, that you will both be mine," he had said, "but I cannot take you with me yet, because I think only my speed will save me from The Ugly One."

"They will not still be there," Benni said, when Baringa told him his plans and that he was going to leave Dawn with him. "They would surely move down into the creek when the wind got really rough."

"They may have stayed," Baringa replied, "and I must see."

Benni rocked back and forth on his strong tail.

"They are all the same, every one of them – his grandsire, his dam and now himself – they must seek danger. Thowra's capture of Golden made all that trouble with Man, now *this* colt must find the filly that is the hidden treasure of the southern mountains. Ah well, that is the way of the silver horses." He tapped Baringa's nose. "Go then, for there is no stopping you, and trust to your marvellous speed. Do not let The Ugly One know that it is from here that you came."

They watched Baringa cross the stream where the darkness of night still seemed to lie. They watched him leaping lightly from shelf to shelf – the white moth flying up the cliff and getting smaller, smaller, smaller. Then they could barely see him. He mingled with the windracked clouds and vanished over the edge.

The forest on the high plateau strained in the tearing wind, leaves glittering, streaming, straining, flying. Baringa was glad to be among the trees, though, because he had felt as if he would be blown off the cliff. Here at least the trees would stop him being lifted bodily. He went trotting quietly along, in and out between the candlebarks and twisted snowgums, not really knowing what he intended to do if he found the lovely, mysterious filly and The Ugly One, but only knowing that he must try.

He thought that, if they were still on the high plateau, it was likely they had gone down the side of it as much out of the wind as possible, so he started to edge off the top, but, even as he did so, a movement far ahead caught his eye – a flash of white, a silver tail.

They were there, he was sure, racing round and round through the trees and playing in the wind!

Suddenly it was almost all Baringa could do to stop himself galloping to join them. With every pulse throbbing with excitement, he slid behind one tree and then another, getting closer and closer to where they played.

Then there was a flash of white dashing towards him.

Baringa froze behind a white ribbongum, as there was no scrub in which to hide. The wind picked up his mane and tossed it, blew out his glorious tail like a pennant.

He was seen! Anyway what use was there in trying to hide?

He drew himself rearing up, and, for the first time in his life, was conscious of his beauty and his strength.

The white and silver filly, the Hidden One, propped to a standstill and stared. For a second Baringa saw her, but with a scream of rage the stallion leapt in front of her, but then he, too, stood silent in amazement at the sight of the young silver horse. Then he came swiftly, menacingly forward.

The devil seized Baringa! He leapt to one side, he dodged round the trees. He leapt behind The Ugly One. For one wild instant his nose touched the soft nose of the lovely filly, and then he swung away before the stallion's striking hoof could touch him.

He galloped and dodged, propped and swung. He even dared a glancing blow at the heavy bay shoulder. He galloped again, swung round quite close to the filly, then away again with a kick of his heels that met bay hide. Galloping, galloping, dodging, biting, kicking, he always headed towards Quambat.

There were miles to go and he did not know the country, so he realised that he must gallop away before he got very tired. After a while he drew further ahead, stopped, gave a clear neigh to the lovely filly, and knew, with satisfaction, that his voice sounded like a stallion's, not just a young colt's.

"I will return," he told her. "Someday you will be mine." Then he galloped, swift as a shaft of early light, and was gone from their sight.

Search though he did, The Ugly One could not find him.

'This Horse Becomes Crazy'

It was a hard winter without much snow, and frost following frost. If the frost did not lie white on the ground, and the ice cover the pools, the cold wind cried across the mountains.

Baringa and Dawn, with the two kangaroos, were most often at Quambat, but sometimes they would vanish for days at a time, and then Lightning wondered where they went.

Because of the whispers amongst other young stallions of a beautiful white filly, and because of the story of the mare that had vanished, he grew very curious, but he was not of a wandering nature, and perhaps he realised that he did not know enough to get himself about in a strange country or to save himself, should any stronger horse wish to fight him.

Baringa only dared seek the white filly when snow was falling.

In all the rest of the winter he only saw her three times. On the third time a little snow had fallen, late one afternoon, and he and Dawn had wandered from the Quambat to the head of The Ugly One's creek. As night fell the clouds cleared away and the fierce frost set in again. Baringa and Dawn crept together under some rocks, trying to warm themselves.

When the first faint light came, the world was cast in cold silver, and against silver snow and silver ice, there was a vision of beauty – a filly cast in the same cold silver. Just then the stallion called her and she vanished away as though she had never been there.

Baringa was sure she had been gazing at them, and he wondered whether she wished to come with them.

Try as he might, in the weeks that followed, he did not see her again.

He and Dawn were both very restless once more, and all the other horses were wandering more, fighting more, playing more. Then suddenly, one day, it was spring time. A warm wind blew, melting ice and snow; suddenly the trees looked more alive, the grass and bushes seemed to reach upwards and no longer looked flattened, and there were birds everywhere. A spray of sarsaparilla on a bank became purple in the warmth of the sun.

Lightning began to be with Dawn and Baringa too much. Baringa had a feeling that he was always imperceptibly edging Dawn away, and yet he could never see him doing it.

Benni watched them all quizzically. He was not surprised when Baringa nipped him gently on the shoulder one night, and headed off towards The Pilot.

Benni and Silky and the joey, now quite big and hopping along on its own, went to the top of The Pilot Ridge with them and then said goodbye, for they would go off for a while into the wild bush. The young horses were left alone in their silver forest.

Benni looked back once and saw them – a young silver stallion and silver filly framed by their silver trees, looking most beautiful, and he raised his little paw as though he would salute beauty.

"Baringa starts to conquer his kingdom," Benni said softly to Silky, "but he will have much strife before he is king of them all," and he turned south-eastward.

Baringa and Dawn stayed for several fine and lovely days on The Pilot Ridge, racing and playing in the warm sunshine, galloping, dancing, bucking, rearing, more and more filled with life and joy as the spring grass grew and gave them the great strength of the mountains.

When rain came, and the wild spring storms, they sought shelter lower down, but did not go back to the Quambat – Baringa was taking no risk of Lightning making any real effort to steal Dawn. Another year must go by before he could be at all sure of keeping her for himself. Anyway, life held too much joy for him and Dawn, alone, stallion and mare.

Baringa had several fights with other horses of his own age, and some with horses that were older. He soon learnt that his speed and agility more than made up for his lack of strength and weight. He loved a fight. He would dance on the tips of his hooves, silver mane and tail swirling, flying, catching every beam of light, and a power went from the land to him, through the tips of those dancing hooves. They struck sparks from the rocks, and the strength of the rocks was his. His hooves sprang from the snowgrass, and all the resilience of the snowgrass was his. His hooves beat, staccato, on the bare earth. . . . He was the mountains' and they were his – the young stallion in all his glory.

As soon as he saw an older stallion in the distance, Baringa would quietly lead Dawn away through the thickness of bush, or into a dense mat of tea tree. He knew that Dawn was as beautiful as a ray of the rising sun, a prize for any horse.

As the spring grew hotter and drier, and Baringa grew stronger and more and more confident, in spite of all his happiness he kept thinking of the Hidden Filly. After all it is the way of the wild stallion to have a herd of mares, and Baringa knew that some day he must try to capture the Hidden Filly, or perhaps die in the attempt.

He and Dawn went one night to the creek which ran into their Secret Canyon, the gentle valley of swamps and tea tree where he had first seen the track of that other silver filly. They slid quietly amongst the trees, hiding, yet seeking, wondering if there would be sign or sound of the one for whom they sought.

The valley seemed empty of all except the wombats by night, and the birds by day – the thrushes' song, the pardalottes' warble, the cry of the kurrawongs to the spring dawn.

There was a strange loneliness.

They went down to their Secret Canyon, where the grass grew thick and sweet, and the spring stream ran swiftly.

During their second night there, a storm came roaring over the mountains. Baringa stirred from half sleep to hear the same noise that had disturbed them in the winter, a wild neigh echoing, first from the top of the Canyon, then from the lower end, then rolling round and round, keening on the wind. The two young horses woke with their skins creeping cold.

Unable to hold back till morning, Baringa led Dawn over the black swirling stream whose waters they could barely see in the night, and whose rocks were invisible. Then they climbed up and up the cliff, cloaked by darkness and buffeted by the ever-veering wind.

All the way Baringa's coat seemed to creep and the hair stand on end. He knew he was going into great danger – and taking Dawn into danger too, yet it was thrilling, exciting, wonderful. Go on, he must! Perhaps he would see the lovely filly. Perhaps he would have to fight The Ugly One – and get a great beating – perhaps he was far faster than The Ugly One.

Dawn followed him, gay-hearted, light-footed, daring the wind, daring the horses ahead.

When they came to the cliff top the cold wind hit them with all its force. Apart from the cry of the storm in the trees, there was no sound of bird or beast. Baringa suddenly knew he must be very, very quiet, very careful. He was afraid, but the strangest elation seized him. He was floating through the air, silent and light, and Dawn was coming like a zephyr of air behind him.

Cold, cold, the wind tore at them. The trees, the branches, the leaves lashed and streamed in the wind. The wind's voice filled the air, and yet there was the emptiness of no other sound. Silently the young horses flowed through the night, on, on, hither and thither, seeking and seeking – and finding nothing. Yet Baringa felt sure The Ugly One and the Hidden Filly were on the plateau. "I will call her the Moon, when she is mine," he thought. Then suddenly he was certain they were near.

He stood still, letting the long hair in his ears, the very hair of his coat, his sensitive nose, tell him where they were. Then he moved forward, drifting across the wind without sound.

They were there! They were sleeping in the lee of a heap of rocks. The Ugly One just a dark sleeping shadow, but, in his eagerness, it seemed to Baringa that the filly almost shone in the night.

He could see her mane lifting in the wind and her long tail flying out to one side. He could see the lovely shape of her – a little higher, a little bigger than when he had first seen her.

Perhaps he could slide between them and take her away!

He nipped Dawn gently to tell her to stay back, then, walking on hooves of thistledown, he stepped between them and started edging the filly away from the stallion with nose, with shoulder.

He was between them before she woke. Then her eyes opened, and she stared at him, her muscles suddenly rigid.

Baringa waited a moment and then nosed her gently away from the sleeping bay stallion.

The filly was obviously very frightened and did not know what to do. Baringa pushed her again, she moved, but as she moved he felt the bay stirring in his sleep. More urgently he pushed his nose against her and stepped after her himself, as quietly as a snowflake drifting through the night.

The filly kept looking fearfully back.

Then suddenly there was a half snort as the bay stallion woke.

Baringa and the filly froze into absolute stillness. Perhaps he might not wake completely, never miss her. . . . Baringa did not even breathe.

The wind blew more wildly and there was a sharp splatter of hail. Another snort! The hail had really woken the bay!

Then Baringa knew what he had done! Not only had he risked his own life and risked losing his beautiful Dawn, but he would probably be the cause of the filly receiving fierce punishment, for the roar that the bay stallion gave was a roar of wildest fury.

The filly shrank back, terrified, and the bay hurtled past her, kicking at her savagely as he passed.

Baringa heard her sudden little squeal of pain and fear and, without thought of how he could hope to win, he sprang forward.

He met the bay, chest on, and was nearly knocked over. Suddenly there were flailing hooves all around him, teeth ripped at him . . . and the hail came lashing down.

Round and round and round the two stallions spun, rearing, struggling. Baringa felt that he would never get his breath again. He gasped and choked.

The bay stallion was blind with anger. Baringa felt the horror of his fury, and felt himself almost shivering at the mad screams.

"This horse becomes crazy," he thought, and also he knew that he was very strong, because the bay struck downwards on to his off shoulder, and it felt as if a tree had fallen on him.

Pain leapt from his shoulder to his ears, leapt down his back, and down his slender leg.

The bay knew he had struck Baringa very hard, and, screaming wildly, came to finish him off. Baringa dodged as though nothing had happened and then reared up, slashing with his unhurt leg. His hoof cut into flesh.

The bay leapt in mad fury.

It was only this blind fury – and the wind and the hail – that saved Baringa. The bay was completely stupid with rage – sightless and senseless.

Even though his off foreleg and shoulder were hurting him constantly, Baringa managed to dodge and strike – to keep himself out of range and yet spring in and bite – and all the time the wind pushed and shoved the two horses, and the hail and rain beat down. An unusually sharp blast nearly knocked Baringa over as he reared. His hind legs trembled as he steadied himself. Then he had to drop on to all four legs if he wished to remain upright. In a moment the wind was taking them, twisting them, driving them, throwing them towards the edge and the cliffs and screes, down the side of the high plateau.

Baringa found Dawn beside him, and she was calling:

"Come, come!"

He could not even see the other filly. He caught a glimpse of the dark shape of the bay crashing among scrub and bushes at the very edge, and only just stopping himself from being blown over, but there was no sign of the other. An even stronger blast of wind tore at them. Now the fight was against the wind, to get across it, and get away from the cliff. Dawn called again, urgently.

Baringa was becoming very lame, even so he could not go to the safety of their Secret Canyon, without trying to find the filly whom he would call the Moon, but he did not find her.

At last, exhausted, and so lame that he could barely go down the cliff with safety, he led Dawn home.

It was in the wildness of this night that Thowra chose to leave *his* Secret Valley and come out into the mountains.

'The Fight to the Finish is for Me'

It was a night so wild that no one would see him. Old Whiteface would be sleeping below a thick tree – that pale strawberry mare, alone of Whiteface's herd, would know he was
coming. Brother Storm might expect him, of course, and
Cirrus, down at Quambat, might know that on the wings of
the wind her horse, the wind, would come.

O glory, glory! He would leap up over the edge of the cliff;
he would gallop before the wind and the hail – hidden by the
storm, made trackless by the rain. He, the son of Bel Bel,
would gallop through his kingdom again. What joy there was
in the swirling air, in the sting of the hail! He went swiftly
through the wild night, leaping over tree trunks, every muscle
strong and resilient as a spring!

As the winter had ended and the snow gone, except from
the tops, the men and the weird machines had come back to
the Crackenback Valley. Thowra saw with amazement that
the wide road had reached up to Dead Horse Gap, cutting
quite deeply into the lovely snowgrass hillside, so that a horse,
walking along it, snuffling and pawing, had to jump to get up
to the hut and the yards – the yard where Golden had been.
Thowra snuffed round the hut, as he and Storm had done so
long ago.

He was glad to turn, to jump down the bank and gallop
away, for this well-known place was no longer his, and he
raced on, thinking eagerly of Stockwhip Gap and the Quambat, of the mares and horses he was going to meet.

The real savagery of the storm hit him while he was in the
Cascades. He tossed the hail out of his mane and forelock and
let himself be driven by the wind. Hail he had seen before in
the Cascades – not just hail but knife-sharp ice, flying through
the air, covering the ground, but that ice came from the south.
This was a fierce spring storm, not a tornado, and Thowra
could run wild with it.

It was because he was galloping with joy through the storm
and thinking of what lay ahead, that he did not immediately
feel the presence of other horses.

The ice-cold wind destroyed scent and sound, but suddenly

he knew that there were horses close. Then his hoof touched fresh droppings and he slackened his wild pace.

He could see nothing, smell nothing, hear nothing through the driving rain and hail. The wind seemed almost solid, but, blown and torn by this wind, there came a neigh.

"Brother of the wild night, here am I!"

"Storm!" he thought, and threw up his head to answer: "Brother, it is I!" and he swung in the direction from which the neigh had come, sure where Storm was, though the neigh had been taken and twisted by the wind.

Storm stood beneath an old, gnarled snowgum – a number of mares round him or quite close. Thowra could feel that they were there, more than he could see them, and the scent of Storm he knew as well, or better, than he knew the scent of Boon Boon and Golden. Even through the hail and the rain he got it, the scent of his beloved half-brother, the scent that had gone with him on all the wild, exciting days and nights up on the Ramshead Range, down on the Crackenback, or The Brindle Bull, or Paddy's Rush's Bogong.

This was a wild, exciting night too. Thowra was heading south.

A few new-born foals woke from sleep and stood wondering at the sound of play, in the hail and the rain, wondering at the shadowy forms of the stallions rearing around each other, cavorting, bucking. Even the foals must have felt the current of excitement that went through the herd.

"The Silver Stallion is here – Thowra, the wind."

A tiny silver foal whinnied and then slept again. At last the stallions ceased their game.

"So, my brother!" said Thowra. "You could not stay away from your Cascade Valley in the spring!"

"No," Storm answered, "but soon we must go further south again, and just let old Whiteface know that we are still alive."

"Yes, you must," said Thowra. "Men are already at Dead Horse Gap, now the snow has gone. As for Whiteface – I will tell him tonight! Let us meet at Stockwhip Gap, when I return from Quambat. Have you heard anything of Baringa and Lightning?"

"There is a whisper," Storm said, "that Baringa has vanished with the coming of the spring. Baringa perhaps has the wisdom of your dam, Bel Bel."

Thowra blew softly through his nose as though he were

amused at something. Then he shook the hail from his coat, touched his nose to Storm's, looked once at the mare with the silver foal – and was gone.

"Thowra, the wind," the herd whispered. "The wind, the wind."

Thowra hurtled on through the night, with the hail and the wind in his mane, the great, vibrating sound of the storm in his ears – the great, vibrating pulse of the mountain spring beating through him.

The climb out of the Cascade Valley slowed him up, and the narrow winding track through scrub and bush along the side of the hill beyond the Gap. When that track got out into the open glades, between the gnarled and wind-pressed snow-gums, it was time to go slowly and quietly, time to be invisible and learn who was there before they knew of his presence.

Whiteface would be somewhere close, sheltering over the edge towards the Charcoal Range.

Thowra went down the little snowgrass valley in which Whiteface had been grazing, the first time they had met.

Presently he could hear the movements of horses, restless and disturbed by the wildness of the night. Old Whiteface's herd must be close.

Just as Baringa had, he floated on the wind in among the horses. At one moment he was not there and then he was, the half-shining shape of a horse made of stardust, or moonlight, or the magic of snow. There was one trembling nose touching his in the darkness. The pale roan mare, who would follow him to the end of the mountains if only she was asked – she knew he was there.

Thowra nipped her gently on the wither, but he was trying with every sense to find out where Whiteface was standing. Then he thought what fun it would be for Whiteface to wake and open his eyes with the dawn, and find him there: so he stayed beside the pale mare.

Presently he felt something bumping against him, and saw in the black, wild night, a foal made of stardust or moonlight.

Morning slowly began to break. Thowra waited. Whiteface was surely going to be pleased to see him.

Whiteface was, in fact, so pleased to see him that he forgot that Thowra had given him a very good beating, and rushed at him with rage.

Thowra danced out into a little patch of early light. He

98

jumped up and down, felt the good snowgrass under his hooves. He threw up his great silver-maned head and cried out his joy to the hills and the sun.

The light-coloured mare watched every lithe and lovely move he made. Her little silver foal hid himself behind her legs.

Thowra side-stepped each time Whiteface rushed at him – side-stepped, danced, sprang hither and thither, and the sun crept up over the mountains to make a fine early morning. This time it was not only the light strawberry mare who watched him. All the mares of the herd stared at the glorious silver horse – and each wished that he, with his dancing hooves, his tossing, silver mane, his rippling muscles, had chosen her instead of the pale strawberry mare.

Whiteface was becoming exhausted again. Soon he might collapse.

"Stop!" Thowra suddenly commanded. "Enough!"

The strawberry mare came diffidently out towards him, the foal trotting beside her.

In the sunlight, Thowra noticed that the little colt's ears were marked with pale roan.

"Dilkara," he said. "That is what he should be called. 'The Rainbow'. He is a fine colt. And you," he said to the mare, "I will call Koora, sweet, and next time I come I will take you to run with Baringa and Cloud, out at Quambat but this time I must gallop free, and the colt is too young."

For a night and a day Thowra roamed the country between Stockwhip Hill and The Lookout with the lovely little mare and her foal. And the mare watched him all the time, watched him prancing in the sunlight or standing high on the rocks, silver hair lifting in the breeze. She thought that she would train Dilkara to be strong and wise, just as Bel Bel had trained Thowra, his magnificent sire, so that she and her foal could follow him south – over the hills, over the hills, wild and free with the Silver Stallion. The young mare threw her head in the air and did a few graceful, dancing steps, and found Thowra prancing beside her. Their feet brushed through the golden and brown flowering shrubs, the little dog violets. A pool reflected them – the Silver Stallion against a blue spring sky, the pale roan mare and her silver foal.

When Thowra left he went off through the mountain ash, over the Moyangul River, along the lovely open valleys, travelling by night in case the cattlemen were bringing out their herds of Herefords.

He did not see Son of Storm – if he had he might have learnt some of the things he wished to know. He saw no emus, nor did he see Benni and Silky. He did see a curl of smoke going up from the Tin Mine huts – up against the stars above the Ingegoodbee Valley.

He crossed the divide on to the Tin Mine Creek. There were two or three hours of darkness left – he would not bother about Steel. He would go on through the mild spring night to the Quambat, find Cirrus, find his son and his grandson. So the night hid him and only the light of the stars sometimes showed the froth and foam of his mane, the flash of his tail.

A mopoke hailed him once – no cry to warn of danger, only a greeting on a spring night to the horse who was king of the mountains.

The sky was just becoming bright when he reached the Quambat. He came to the top of the flat and stood still, within the fringe of trees, his eyes, alone, moving, as he looked for the herds.

Soon he made out Cloud and Mist beneath one tree. They were just waking. Cirrus was not far from them.

Way down the flat was a herd of roans, and then out of the trees, near the junction of the two small creeks, Lightning stepped, followed by Goonda and a creamy foal.

There was no sign of Baringa.

Already Cirrus knew Thowra was there – for the Silver Brumby was a horse whose very presence sent a current of excitement through the air. She came quietly towards him, moving from one patch of trees to another, knowing that he might want to be unseen for the moment.

"Where is Baringa?" Thowra asked after they had greeted each other.

Cirrus looked far off, as though she would pierce the secrets of mountain and bush.

"That I cannot tell you for certain," she answered. "He went when the spring came, he and Benni and Silky. It was wise of him because he could not hope to keep Dawn. Lightning wanted her."

"Where do you think they went?"

"Well, they went to The Pilot – the emus told me, but the emus also whispered of a lovely silver filly whom no one ever

100

sees, somewhere away towards the great river . . ."

"I see . . ." Thowra murmured.

"Baringa takes after you," said Cirrus.

Thowra thought of the proud-stepping colt, who was all fire.

"I may learn something from Lightning," he said.

Cirrus walked down the flat with him to see Lightning.

Lightning was not quite easy when he saw Thowra. If he had protected the younger Baringa, instead of trying to take his mare, Baringa would have been at Quambat to greet his grandsire in the spring.

Thowra was enjoying himself too much to bother to get angry, and, anyway, if he wanted to find out about Baringa he would ask later.

He admired the foal. He praised Goonda. Eventually it was from Goonda that he heard that the other young horses told tales of a mare that had vanished, of her silver filly, and of a stallion whose nature was of fury and madness. And he learnt a rough idea of the direction in which the Hidden Filly's country lay. He also learnt that Baringa had indeed been gone since the first day of spring, and not returned even once, so he did not expect him to turn up.

Thowra decided not to leave Quambat in a hurry. He had no wish to make all the others more curious about Baringa and about this beautiful, barely seen filly. Better that Baringa became more or less forgotten until he had attained his full growth. He, Thowra, would seek him soon, but when he did so it must seem as though he was returning to his own herd.

When he left, he went in the darkness and silence of the night, and only Cirrus knew he had gone.

At the head of the creek where Baringa had first seen the hoofmark like Dawn's, and the silver hair, he waited till it grew light, and then began his search.

All day Thowra searched. The little valley was strangely empty of horses. Birds sang – thrushes, pardalottes, tree-creepers, kurrawongs – a few kangaroos hopped through the bush, but he saw no horses, and though he did see some fairly old tracks, he did not really know the shape of Dawn's hoof, far less the fact that the Hidden Filly's was identical. Baringa's track, he was sure, was not there. If Baringa had travelled that valley recently, he had left no mark.

Thowra might have gone on then, down the creek till he

101

came to the start of cliffs and gorge that would surely have made him think of a secret valley, but he heard a wild neigh from somewhere, way up on the high, lonely country between him and the great river that lay to the west. That one wild neigh ringing through the half-light of evening, called Thowra to the high plateau.

It was night before he was right up in the moving air and the moving trees of that lonely plateau on the edge of the world. No sound called him on and yet he had heard it – that wild-sounding neigh – and he knew there was a stallion somewhere.

The night was not a good time to search through unknown country for an unknown horse – a horse that had a strange sound of madness in his neigh – but Thowra went on in his great strength, unafraid.

He heard nothing and he saw nothing.

"Surely I did hear that stallion's neigh," he thought, "that is what called me up here," but there was nothing.

Then suddenly he came on a stallion's rolling hollow, and there were signs of horses having been there some hours ago. Thowra began to wonder if he, with his silver hide, had been seen, and if the other horse had crept away, but there was something in that neigh which had not sounded like a horse that would creep away.

Thowra felt a ripple of discomfort go down the hair on his back as he thought of the sound of that stallion cry.

Still he did not find the horse.

At last he came to the northernmost end of the plateau, where it dropped in sharp cliffs. There he backed into a wedge-shaped space between two rocks, and slept till it was almost light. When he woke, he found himself looking out over a great chasm, a valley still filled with darkness, below cliffs that dropped steep and straight.

Thowra looked with interest, then he moved cautiously out of his cleft, enough to see the surrounding bush. There was no sign of anyone. He moved out further and there was still no sign nor sound. Then he went to the edge and peered over into the depth where the night still lay, wondering what was below . . . and then there was a sound behind him.

He turned just in time to see a furious, slab-headed, bay stallion leap at him.

There was not a moment to get away from the edge or to

step to either side. He only had time to dig in his hooves, brace himself forward to meet the force of the other's spring.

He saw the red nostrils, the blood-shot whites of the animal's eyes – and knew that he was mad.

Then there was only the terrible swaying back and forth on the edge and Thowra had the feeling of space touching him as they swayed.

He knew he had the advantage of weight and strength, the bay had the advantage of his leap – the disadvantage of his mad fury. Thowra pressed him back and back from the edge.

It might have been a simple thing to step sideways and let that mad horse sail off, fall, fall, fall into space, but Thowra was only interested in driving him away, and right away, so that he could study the cliffs and the valley below when the light crept into it.

He never saw the beautiful white filly who watched from among the trees, and by the time he had driven off the mad bay stallion, she had retreated out of sight.

The bay was in such a fury that he seemed to have no realisation of his danger, no realisation of the great superiority of the silver horse. In the end Thowra not only had to drive him away, but give him quite a blow on the head to calm him down.

Thowra returned to the cliff.

He could see a shelf just below the top and decided to wait there till there was sufficient light right down in the valley! There he would be invisible from the plateau. He jumped down almost as lightly as he had jumped, years before, into his own Secret Valley, and there, on the shelf, set hard by the heat of the sun, was the mark of Baringa's near forefoot, deeply indented.

Thowra sniffed at it and felt a tingle of excitement go through him. Baringa had been here and had been hurrydown the face of the cliff, and possibly was lame. Soon there would be enough daylight for him to pick a way down that cliff face too.

Thus it was that Dawn, who had heard the noise of the fight and kept looking up at the cliff even long after there was silence, saw a silver horse descending.

Her heart leapt with fear – thinking of Lightning. Then she saw that this horse was not Lightning but looked more like Baringa – Baringa who was there beside her. She looked from him to the horse far up on the cliff, then drew back behind

103

some rocks, nickering softly to call Baringa back too.

"Who is that on the cliff?" she whispered.

Baringa jumped nervously and looked up.

"Ah," he said, his coat losing the staring look which fright gave it. "Who should it be but Thowra, the wind."

When Thowra got to the creek crossing, Baringa limped out to greet him, Dawn following nervously behind.

Thowra came through the high water that boiled and swirled over the boulders as if water, as well as the air, was his element. He bowed his head ceremoniously towards Dawn, touched Baringa's nose with his, and said:

"Who lamed you, O my grandson?"

"The Ugly One, we call him," Baringa answered. "It is nothing. In a day or so I will be right."

"That must be he, whom I have just met," said Thowra.

"Did you fight him?" Baringa asked quickly.

"He's not much hurt, just a little sillier than usual," Thowra answered cheerfully.

"The fight to the finish with him is for me," Baringa said.

Thowra looked at him with one eye rather more closed than the other.

"Your Ugly One is big and strong, but he is also mad. Take care he doesn't kill you and himself at once, which is what he has just nearly done to me."

"I know already that he becomes mad with rage."

Thowra opened both eyes.

"Does the mysterious white filly run with him?" he asked.

Questions in the Wind

The white filly . . . the white filly . . . Who has seen the white filly? Where does she run? The wind whispered the questions, the sound of them rustled in the snowgum leaves, murmured in the streams; questions that teased the young stallions of Quambat Flat all through the spring and the start of the summer.

Baringa knew the answers.

Lightning would have liked to know the answer to another question – where was Baringa?

He knew that Baringa must be all right because otherwise Thowra would have returned, full of anger, to find out what he, Lightning, knew about him, but Thowra had returned once again, in that spring, blazing with life, and he and Cirrus had vanished even farther south into the unknown and mysterious country of the Limestone Creek, perhaps to the Cobras, who knew? Then Cirrus was back at the Quambat one morning, and Thowra was no longer there.

Lightning began to wander rather farther from Quambat. All the horses sought fresh pastures because, in the unusual heat of the early summer, the grass that had come up in the spring was drying off very quickly. There had been so little rain and snow in the winter that now the mountains were dry.

The hot north wind blew all day and the cold south wind blew each night, whispering those never-answered questions over the mountains. The land became drier and drier. Quambat Flat was brown, dusty. The hollow sound was more noticeable beneath galloping hooves. At sunset it was as though the very bones of the land were showing, touched by the fiery red glow. Then the divine scent of the eucalypts, whose leaves were bruised by the wind and burnt by the sun all day, blew everywhere.

Baringa's lameness had at last worn off, and night after night he roamed the high plateau searching, searching, or took Dawn to the Tin Mines, or even up on to The Pilot. He grew bigger and stronger, and always more nimble, always faster.

Lightning was restless, as no young stallion really should be, once spring is past, when he has a mare and foal to look after. He and Goonda and the foal sought grass as did the other horses, but they also sought the answers to the questions: The white filly. Where does she run? Baringa? Where is he?

Perhaps Benni might be somewhere upon The Pilot, perhaps the emus might appear if they wandered along the soaks at the creek heads. Lightning led Goonda and the foal up to the very head of the Quambat Creek, one head of the great Murray River. There, though strange horses flitted through the forest, he saw never a sign of Baringa or Dawn, and the country above, leading up on to The Pilot, was too rough for the foal.

Perhaps Baringa was up on The Pilot. . . . He led them by winding brumby tracks around the base of the mountain till they were almost on the head of the Tin Mine Creek. So far they had not been molested, but now, with every step, Lightning began to think of Steel.

He swung off the track and climbed over a ridge so that he was on the headwaters of Dale's Creek, in the soft valley where the wind barely whispered those questions – there where the answers might be learnt.

The tea tree flowered as though it were the snow that had not fallen to refresh the springs and bogs. The birds sang, but otherwise there was the same strange silence that had greeted Thowra.

Lightning was uneasy and yet he stayed near the head of the creek for several days, grazing with his mare and foal. He insisted on silence, and Goonda became more and more uneasy herself. The little foal missed his companions at Quambat.

Then one night Lightning woke in the star-bright darkness. He did not know why he had woken, and he seemed to see in his eyes as though it were real, the vision of a young silver stallion and a young silver mare.

There was nothing there now, and yet the two could not have been a dream. Lightning walked forward slowly, eyes trying to pierce the darkness.

Goonda woke nervously.

"There is no one," she said. "For whom do you search?"

"There was someone there, I am sure," said Lightning, but the image of the silver stallion and the silver mare was fading from his eyes.

Neither Lightning nor Goonda slept again that night, and in the morning Lightning began ceaselessly wandering to and fro, searching for grass and searching, searching, searching, for he felt sure within himself that he had woken to see Baringa and Dawn and that they had vanished. Perhaps he had got the answer to one of those questions.

There was some nourishing grass up a little hanging valley where the spring still ran. They wandered up, eating as they went, Goonda keeping near the trees, her feet brushing among pale vanilla lilies, her skin creeping with fear, but she was too uneasy to enjoy the good grass.

Ahead there was a patch of rank green grass. Lightning went up to it and stopped, snorting.

Step by step Goonda, with the little foal at her heels, went to join him and see what it was, knowing that that grass could

106

only mean that here some animal had died, and when she saw the skeleton of a horse, she swung away, back to the friendly trees.

"Come," she said to Lightning. "Come away."

Lightning was wondering, but Goonda gave him no peace.

"Come," she said. "Come. Take our foal from here. This is no place for us."

"I do not know," said Lightning, "I do not know. Perhaps near here we might find Baringa."

"I tell you we must go back towards Quambat where we will be safe from evil," Goonda said, and she would not be quiet till he left off searching through the bush, trying to find tracks, trying to find some sign. He was not as sharp-eyed as Baringa and he found no silver hair.

At last Goonda prevailed, and, with many a backward glance, Lightning took them back towards Quambat, but that vision of the silver stallion and the silver mare which had perhaps been in his own eyes and not in reality, haunted Lightning. Night after night he woke thinking he had seen them and so one day he left Goonda and the foal grazing near Cloud, and went off to the head of Dale's Creek.

Unlike Baringa, Lightning had never wandered on his own. Baringa belonged to the bush almost like the kangaroos did, but Lightning had never heeded Thowra's or Boon Boon's teaching, so he did not observe things he might have observed, nor did he manage to keep himself hidden in the way he should have, even though he kept in the trees.

He had not gone far when he began to feel as jumpy as Goonda had been when they were there before. He felt that eyes were watching him. Every moving zephyr of air was the exhaled breath of an invisible horse.

It was one of those mornings that are tense and still before a big wind comes. Everything told the bush creatures that something was going to happen, and nothing could really bear to be still even though the heat was great.

At midday, as the gusts of hot wind blew from the north, seven black cockatoos flew crying, screaming, up Dale's Creek.

Thowra, with Koora and Dilkara, on the ridge between the Tin Mine Creek and Dale's Creek, heard them. Baringa and Dawn, who had been unable to stand the tense atmosphere, and had left the Canyon, heard them. The Ugly One and the Hidden Filly heard them as they came down off the high

107

plateau. Lightning heard them from the gap between Pilot Creek and Dale's Creek, and felt the sweat of fear break on his coat. And the black cockatoos, seeing much of what went on, cried aloud to the coming wind.

Silver horses, silver mares, and a silver foal went quietly, proudly stepping through the bush towards Dale's Creek ... quietly, proudly, all unknowing, while the black cockatoos wheeled and flew crying, crying down the valley.

Thowra stood with Koora and Dilkara, sweat dripping off them, high on the ridge above the Secret Canyon. He was wondering which way he would go down, wondering if Baringa were there, wondering who else was close, wondering, listening, *feeling*. Every time the black cockatoos flew over he felt the magnificent excitement of apprehension.

Koora stood close to him so that their coats touched with every breath, receiving the excitement he transmitted. For Koora this was glory – to follow the Silver Stallion over the mountains, to be close to him. She raised her head to the touch of the blistering hot sun, the touch of the furnace wind. Her mane lifted, her ears pricked. She was alive with joy and ready to follow wherever he led.

For some reason which the wind told him, or the birds, or

the blazing sun, Thowra turned towards the gentler valley of Dale's Creek.

The black cockatoos wheeled again, crying. Koora, her shoulder against Thowra's quarters when he stopped, felt the thrill of excitement leap from him right through her.

It was then that Thowra saw the faintest imprint of the track that he now knew to be Dawn's. It was fresh, and it was headed the way he was going.

The great, sombre cockatoos flew up the valley. The Ugly One who, with the Hidden Filly, had been resting in the shade, broke into a sweat again as their weird screaming called up fear of he knew not what.

Lightning shrank back under cover of the tea tree in the swamps at the head of the creek, but the cockatoos saw everything – everything except a soft grey shadow that was moving through the bush.

Thowra went on and on, perhaps two miles, without seeing another of Dawn's hoofmarks, and not a sign of Baringa, then, all of a sudden, he saw two tracks that he thought were unmistakably Dawn's but ahead of them, on some damp black soil, was the broad, strong hoofmark of a stallion who was not Baringa.

Thowra paused and sniffed at the tracks. There were several more before the damp soil ended in snowgrass, and after that there was only an occasional hollow pressed in the grass. He followed these carefully, thinking that it was undoubtedly Dawn's track, and that she was with a heavy, probably ugly stallion.

The Ugly One! That was what Baringa had called the one who had lamed him. Perhaps this was he! *Was the other track really Dawn's?*

Thowra suddenly changed his course and climbed up the side of the valley a little way so that he would skirt the valley floor. Then he began to walk faster, as fast as Dilkara could go.

Lightning, too, had begun to go faster because he wanted to get his expedition over and done with. He would rather have gone home, but he had to try to find out the answer to those questions, and now it seemed as if the black cockatoos cried the questions aloud.

"White filly . . . White filly . . . Baringa . . . Bar*ing*a?"

At last Lightning became too afraid of being on the valley floor. There he could be attacked from above, below, behind.

109

So he, also, went up on to the side of the valley.

The day grew hotter and hotter. The gusts of wind were more frequent. Baringa and Dawn were hidden in thick tea tree.

The Ugly One and the white filly whom Baringa said he would call the Moon walked up the valley, and they did not take much care to hide, for this was their valley and no one molested them here.

Thowra, hidden by trees as he walked along, kept a watch on the valley floor. *He* saw The Ugly One and he saw the beautiful white filly behind him. *He* saw a movement in a dense mass of tea tree, and, from above, saw a gleam of silver mane, the flicker of an ear, and knew in a sudden flash that Baringa and Dawn were hidden there.

He stood quite still to watch.

The big bay stallion and the strange white filly walked closer and closer to the tea tree. Thowra stood tensely waiting while the hot wind blew. The big bay drew level with the tea tree. The tea tree flew apart and Baringa sprang on to the bay stallion's wither, achieving a tremendous, maddening grip with that one leap.

The bay plunged and shook himself, screaming with anger. He reared, he twisted, and he *yelled*.

Thowra became aware of several things all at once: an increase in the wind, a strangely horrifying scent on the wind, *and* another silver horse below him in the trees, moving towards the unknown white filly.

Lightning!

Thowra began to move down, after first telling Koora and Dilkara to stand still.

He stood in the trees at the side of the valley floor and saw Lightning sneak out close to the white filly who was so like Dawn.

The filly snorted in sudden fright and backed away from him. As he advanced she aimed a kick at him that was definitely a warning, and laid her ears back in anger.

"The next time she will really kick or bite," Thowra thought, but Lightning was not to be put off so easily.

He posed in front of her, showing off all his good looks, and then sidled up to her again, not hurrying because Baringa still had hold of the bay and they were locked together, whirling round and round.

By now the filly was becoming a little nervous as well as angry. She lashed at Lightning's neck with her teeth and then swung around and kicked him fiercely on the shoulder.

"That'll slow you up," thought Thowra.

The mad bay stallion had at last thrown Baringa off and now Baringa was fighting the sort of fight for which, at present, he was most suited. He danced around and darted at his opponent, swift as a sunbeam, then he was away before the heavier horse could touch him, danced again and leapt and darted. The already enraged bay became more and more stupid with his mad fury. They fought on and on, the hot wind drying their sweat, thirst making the bay quieter.

Thowra watched but kept an eye on Lightning too. Lightning was already bleeding from kicks and bites, but the filly, as the afternoon wore on, was becoming really afraid.

Thowra stepped out into the open and did a skirmish round them all. Baringa noticed him, though till then he had not seen Lightning. Even the bay stopped in the middle of a scream and stared, as though at a very bad dream. Then he leapt at Lightning, who was near his filly, just as Baringa leapt at *him*.

Koora, from the safety of the trees, watched the strange sight of the three-sided battle, and Thowra rearing and cavorting around, striking lightly here and there, as though to keep the fight going. Koora, alone, saw the filly, over whom they were fighting drift quietly away. She saw Dawn creep out of the tea tree and touch her nose, but the other filly kept going through the bush rather sadly, as though she were afraid. Koora saw her shy once, but did not see the little grey kangaroo whose sneeze caused her to shy.

The kangaroo hopped quietly into the tea tree beside Dawn.

It was Baringa who first realised the filly had gone. He knew also that, this time, he was not going to be able to beat The Ugly One and, while Lightning and The Ugly One were momentarily locked together, he went round the tea tree and then sank from sight into its dense cover beside Dawn.

Benni tapped him softly on the nose.

"The heat and the wind told me that it was time to come to you, Baringa," he said, "and now there is smoke in the wind."

"Smoke," said Baringa. "What is smoke?"

"Smoke is breathed out by fire," said Benni.

"Wait!" said Benni, with one little forepaw higher than the other. "Watch!"

Baringa and Dawn peered through the tea tree. They could see Lightning and the bay striking at each other, thundering round and round. Then suddenly there was an even madder scream from the bay stallion.

They saw him shake himself free of Lightning and canter, puffing and blowing, along the track up which the Hidden Filly had vanished.

Lightning followed, and the trampled and pawed-up valley was empty. Just then there was an even harder blast of hot wind, and the tea tree parted as Thowra stepped in, quite silently, followed by Koora and the foal, Dilkara.

"Well!" said Thowra. "Who would have expected such an assemblage of the Silver Herd – and Benni, the friend of the Silver Herd!" and as he spoke they could hear the wind moaning up the valley and feel it moving the tea tree.

Baringa noticed the foal with its faint roan colouring on the ears, and Koora's gay pride.

"I came to bring Koora and Dilkara to your secret canyon," said Thowra to his grandson.

Then Benni tapped Thowra's nose.

"Let us go, O Silver Horse! There is too much smoke."

"What could this smoke do to us?" asked Baringa.

Thowra, too, looked towards Benni.

"It means Man," he said questioningly to the kangaroo, "but it is a long way off, isn't it? It comes on the wind."

Benni's little pointed face was solemn.

"This does not mean Man. It may mean fire on the wind. Something tells me . . . It is so hot . . . the bush may light up."

Baringa looked from Benni to Thowra and back again. He did not know what Benni meant and he could see that Thowra did not really know either.

"I have lived longer than you, O Thowra. You have not seen the red flame flying over the grass, or heard it crackle as it leaps into the scrub in the forest or seen the wind take it so that

112

it roars up into the big trees, high, high, red flames roaring. It is fear and it is death," said Benni.

The horses all stood listening and watching him, because Benni with his grey pointed face and dark tipped ears, the rhythmic curve of his body, seemed to be the ancient bush itself, and though they still wondered at what he had said, they knew with certainty, by the trembling nose, the fear in his eyes, that the smell of smoke meant something horrible and terrible.

"I will wake Silky," said Benni, "and we will go to Baringa's canyon. There is plenty of water there, and perhaps there is still green grass."

"Yes, some of the grass is green still," said Baringa, "and, though the creek is low, there is lots of water."

"We must find a deep hole," Benni murmured, and the horses wondered once more.

Baringa sniffed the furnace wind again.

"We must go," said Benni, and Silky, awake now, and looking very nervous, said:

"Quickly! Quickly!"

Baringa kept wondering about that lovely filly whom in his own mind he already called Moon, but he followed Thowra and Benni down the valley because he knew he must take Dawn to safety – if there was safety anywhere.

When they came to the cliffs into the Canyon it was he who led the way down the narrow shelves, and leaping on to rocky outcrops, looking back to make sure that Koora and Dilkara followed safely.

The little foal was nervous and its roan ears continually flickered, its nose trembled and twitched, but it never hung back, just came along obediently and with courage.

Baringa recognised this quality of courage in the foal and in its dam who stepped so proudly behind Thowra.

Several times the wind almost blew the foal off the cliffs and the air was not good to breathe.

Baringa felt as though he were choking, and when he reached the floor of the Canyon he led Dawn to his favourite drinking place. The mare and foal joined them immediately, and Thowra followed. They sank their noses into the cool water, but Baringa could not forget the choking air, could not forget Benni's fear, could not forget that the Hidden Filly – Moon – had gone off into the bush.

113

He raised his head from the water, and as his nostrils dried and there was no moisture to filter the choking smoke, he knew he must go. He turned to Benni.

"Will you look after Dawn while I go to try to find Moon – the silver filly?" he said.

"And Koora and Dilkara while I return to my herd?" Thowra asked.

"They will stay here with me," answered Benni, "but hasten, and remember that in water you are safe from fire."

Koora's eyes followed Thowra as he climbed up the cliffs on his way to the Tin Mine Creek, but Baringa did not see her because he was climbing as quickly as he could on to the high plateau, his silver hide becoming streaked with sweat.

It was on the high plateau he would find Moon, he told himself, and up, up, up he climbed.

The kangaroos and Dawn watched him from below – but the sky was darkening, though night was still hours away, and his outline was hazed and unreal.

For Baringa the world had become unreal too. The smoke-filled air choked him as he gasped for breath while he strained every muscle to climb up quickly. His eyes were sore with the stinging air. There was no relief, no water to drink, here on the cliff, no water in which to sink his nostrils to wash out the smoke.

At last his coat became so wet with sweat that even the hot blast of the wind felt cold against his dripping hair. Baringa had never before known this unreasoning fear that began to grow inside him.

The air grew darker, and the gusts of smoke-laden wind were strong enough almost to blow him off his footholds as he paused, gasping for breath, choking.

He looked back and might have gone down again if it had not been that he thought he heard a neigh. He was sure that Moon was somewhere up there and knew he must get to her and bring her to safety in his Secret Canyon.

At last Baringa scrambled over the top of the cliff, lungs bursting, the smoky breath rasping at his throat – and hid himself among the rocks in which Thowra had slept, so that he could get his breath and look around before anyone saw him. Then, from quite close, forlorn and afraid, torn by the smoke-thick wind, there came a neigh.

Baringa was sure it was the Hidden Filly – alone, except

for a mad stallion, alone to meet whatever terror was coming.

The wind carried flying leaves and twigs now. As Baringa moved out of his rocks one of these leaves fell on a patch of snowgrass at his feet. He looked at it carefully. It was a curled-up frond of bracken such as he had never seen before. It was black. He sniffed at it and it crumbled to pieces. This was the first time he had seen ash.

Then the neigh rang out again. Another frond of burnt bracken brushed by his nose. The unreasoning fear rose up through his body again, but sank because he had something he must do. He must get Moon, and take her to his canyon which, in his imagination, was no longer filled with smoke, but clean and fresh and safe.

He began to jog through the trees in the direction from whence the neigh had come.

The air was thicker with the flying leaves and bracken now, and more dense with smoke so that even a silver horse was no longer gloriously visible. Also the sound of the wind covered the sound of his hooves.

He gulped for breath. . . . If only there were water to drink and with which to clear his nostrils, so that for a moment he could breathe. . . . He trotted on, and the smoke became ever more dense till he felt as if he were groping for his way. It was not like trotting through the night, when his eyes and every sense's magic cunning could pierce a way: *this* darkness was thick, and his eyes streamed from the stinging smoke, the noise of the wind filled his ears and he felt as if he would never hear anything else: the smoke blocked his nose and no other scent could possibly come to him.

He began to think he must have gone too far. Once again he fought down unreasoning terror.

He turned a little east, entering an opening in the forest at its southernmost end. There he stopped to listen and tried to *feel* against the numbing battery of the wind. He looked north, for something was coming.

There was a sudden roar from the ridge between his canyon and the Tin Mine Creek. The smoke parted as if with the force of an explosion, and he could see the shape of the ridge – red, redder far than sunset. Against the red he saw the Hidden Filly.

She was standing, head thrown up, mane and tail wildly streaming in the wind, every line of her body proclaiming

115

terror, and she glowed rose-coloured in the weird and burning light.

Baringa leapt towards her, there was another crackling explosion to the north of them, there was a ghastly scream of uncontrolled fear from the mad bay stallion as he started to gallop away – and the smoke closed down again, darker than any night.

Baringa called then, too, called desperately to the Hidden Filly to come with him, his voice, the voice of a young stallion, rising above the great noise of the fire.

"It is I, Baringa. Come with me!" and with an enormous bound he went across the clearing which he could no longer see, calling her as he leapt.

The bush was ablaze; the bay stallion had galloped ahead of the fire, mad with fear; he must take the filly to safety; and even in that flashing, burning moment, he wondered what had become of Lightning.

The filly had barely moved, being transfixed by the sound of his call, and he found her still standing.

There was no time even to touch noses.

"Quick, follow me," he said, but she hung back because he was leading her across the blazing heat, not away from it, across the force of the wind, the path of the blowing, charred fragments.

"Quick! I know a way to safety!" but he wondered if he did. Was all the bush going to burn around them? Should they run before the fire as The Ugly One had done?

Fear, mad fear went through him, racing like fire on the wind, shaking him. Oh the burning heat, the driving wind, the smoke, the smoke, the acrid, choking air that was no longer breath, the sticks and leaves that burnt the hide as they fell! But there were Dawn, and Benni, back in the Secret Canyon, the only place that was safe.

"Stay right beside me," he called, and could feel her shoulder by his flank as they galloped through the intense heat, the flying ash and burnt leaves.

A blazing stick landed beside them. Fire burst from the scorched ground.

Baringa, with bursting lungs, galloped towards the cliff.

The sky was red above the smoke and yet they were surrounded in darkness. He was suddenly afraid that they would gallop over the edge. They must be nearly there.

116

"Steady," he called, propping almost to a standstill in a few short strides, and then suddenly he felt the edge below him, the terrifying sensation of space.

He turned his head swiftly to the filly, afraid that she might not have been able to stop.

She was trembling beside him.

"We go down these cliffs," he said. "Follow me closely," and he jumped over the edge on to the first shelf. As he looked up to see if she was coming, he saw the dark outlines of three kurrawongs against the red in the sky, and their wind-tossed flight seemed desperate.

"Quick," he cried, and she was behind him in an instant.

Down they went, shaking with fear and exhaustion and lack of breath. The wind tore at them and the leaves and twigs burnt them as they fell.

During an even fiercer, hotter blast, they cowered against the rocks, their foothold narrow and all but invisible.

"It is here," cried the filly, not knowing what "it" was or of what she was so desperately afraid, and her terrified scream was heard far below, because an answering call came out of the deep canyon.

It was Dawn's voice, and because of it Baringa held on to his rocks, while overhead leapt red flame, scorching hair and hide, forcing tears from their eyes, leaving no air to breathe.

All around them was the roar, the crackle, the terrified squeaks and cries of the small things of the bush who might not escape – and the heat, the burning, blistering heat. All they could do was cling to the cliff, cling and cower.

At last it seemed to have passed. Trees above the cliffs were still burning, and some little bushes that grew among the rocks, but the great fire itself had gone roaring on.

Baringa was dizzy for want of air. He could hardly believe he was alive. He turned to look at the filly. She was still there, still alive too, and so blackened that he could hardly recognise her.

He forced some sort of sound from his parched throat, calling Dawn, but the call was not loud enough for her to hear. Presently there came her ringing neigh, desperately calling to know if he still lived, and, try as he might, he could not make a neigh come from his choking throat.

Slowly and painfully, gasping, shaking, Baringa and Moon climbed down the cliff among burning bushes and over

117

blistering rocks, till at last they stumbled into the creek, falling on their knees to drink, and rolling sideways with uttermost exhaustion into the water.

The wind and the fire roared over the mountains, racing and crackling into the leaves of the snowgums, making a blazing torch of the candlebarks, bringing down the giants of the forest – the great mountain ash. The heat shrivelled leaf and flower before the flames burnt them. Fire singed fur and feathers: and the choking smoke left the birds of the air no air to breathe – and air is their element, so many of them could live no longer.

Kangaroos, wallabies, wombats, even some of the possums, knew by an ancient instinct that they must save themselves, and some got into water or the harbour of bare, rock-sheltered earth, but horses went mad with fear and galloped before the flames.

Baringa and Moon were too exhausted to wonder about Thowra or Lightning, or The Ugly One, but Koora kept watching the cliff up which Thowra had climbed, and occasionally she gave a long, lonely neigh. Benni stood beside the stream, his coat drying, his face quite still and sad, only his ears and eyes moving as he listened and watched, and sometimes looked down at the young horses, still lying in the water. He remembered the charred bush of other fires. He had known white heaps of bones that the grass and the scrub did not cover till after the snow had come and gone.

For Thowra, Benni had a great friendship, and Thowra had gone up on to that ridge where the fire first struck.

They waited in the intense heat, white ash still falling, and burning twigs sizzled and hissed as they landed in the stream. No one spoke. There was only the occasional sound of Koora's sad call.

Baringa and Moon got up at last and climbed out of the water, and through the haze of fear, Baringa began to wonder about Lightning, about Thowra, even The Ugly One.

Night came, and the black dark held a thousand red eyes of burning trees, and logs, and stumps, while over and over again there was a sudden flare in the sky as another mountain or ridge burst into flame. The northern sky was red.

The night wore on in silence and fear, but down the dark

118

side of the Canyon, sometimes illuminated by a burning tree, there came a proud horse.

Koora saw him first and her head went up, her ears pricked and she trembled.

He was there, alive, coming slowly down the cliff; returning to her still proud: still the king.

She stepped to meet him, to nuzzle his ears, to snuff nervously at the patches where his hide had been burnt.

Search

Benni, covered in charcoal and ash, the rims of his eyes reddened, hopped carefully down the steep wall of the Secret Canyon. In places the ground was still hot, in places white ash covered embers that burnt his feet and tail. He could see the horses down by the creek. Thowra, Baringa and Moon moved around stiffly. He knew their hooves were sore, knew that the burns on their coats hurt with every movement. Baringa and his little filly were also completely exhausted.

Presently he was hopping towards them, across the flat where the grass was ashy but unburnt.

Thowra raised his head carefully because a burn on his neck hurt.

"What news?" he asked.

"Of Lightning I saw no sign," Benni answered. "Charred death lies beneath the blackened trees, O Thowra – but not Lightning. The bush is burnt for miles, and only the carrion crows are moving."

"I must go, Benni, my friend," said Thowra. "I must know how Storm fared, and I must go to my Secret Valley to see my herd."

"And I," said Baringa, "must search for Lightning." He did not mention The Ugly One.

"You, Baringa, will stay here for today," Benni said. "Then you may search for Lightning."

"That is right," said Thowra. "First, you have brought a new and beautiful mare to your canyon and you cannot leave her straightaway. Secondly, you would be useless, so footsore and tired. I, too, am footsore, but I am not as tired. Rest a day

119

and then go to Quambat – there is Cirrus, also, of whom I would have word."

Baringa looked at his new filly and knew he must stay a day with her. He had the fleeting thought that he would never really feel that she was his until he had found and defeated The Ugly One – if The Ugly One were still living.

There was also Lightning.

"I will stay a day," he said and shuddered because he heard Benni's words again: "Charred death." Quickly he touched Dawn's nose with his, and then Moon's.

Koora went a little way with Thowra. When she returned with her foal Benni said:

"The danger is over now – except the danger from falling trees, and I think Thowra is too wise to be caught thus."

Koora nuzzled her silver foal.

Thowra went slowly upwards, ears twitching, every nerve jumping. The forest would be black and leafless he knew, because it had been black when he came through it to safety last night, but what else would he see? Were many of the animals and the birds burnt – the birds and beasts who had always been friends to a hunted silver horse? If it had not been for a rock overhanging a waterhole he, too, might have been charred death.

Burnt and footsore, he was still magnificently alive.

Near the top all the leaves on the trees and bushes were shrivelled up or burnt, but the fire had gone too quickly for it to burn down into the Canyon. Ash had fallen on to everything and Thowra's coat was soon grey again.

For the last twenty feet of the climb, the crowns of the trees were burnt.

Thowra pulled himself over the top on to the black ridge. There he stood, snorting and trembling. He had come along this ridge in the lurid red and black evening after the fire had raced on and when the ground was hot to his hooves. Now he saw that most of the bush had gone. The biggest trees still smouldered and occasionally flames licked over trunk or branch as the wind fanned embers. The world was black, polished black . . . and utterly silent.

There was no cover for a silver horse.

Thowra backed over the edge of the steep drop to the Canyon and stood among the scorched and ash-covered trees and bushes and wondered what to do next.

120

If the fire had roared over this canyon of Baringa's it had surely passed over his Secret Valley, too, and left Boon Boon, Golden, Kunama and the others unhurt. It was Storm whom he wished to see alive — Storm, his brother of the wild wind who had shared so much of his life. Away to the south there was Cirrus too.

While he stood wondering, Thowra noticed the intense silence.

"Neither bird nor beast moves," he thought, "and there are no leaves left through which the wind may sigh. Perhaps every animal is near water . . ." But he remembered Benni's words, and cold fear touched him, even as he stood in the dry and burning heat. Then he told himself: "If nothing moves, there is nothing to molest me. Surely I may go without cover. Men will come to the Ingegoodbee and the Tin Mine Creek to see if their cattle live, but not yet."

Thowra climbed over the top again, took one more long look to make sure that no one else stood watching, and then started to walk through the black world, through the grim silence.

Wherever he placed his feet he left a hoofmark in ash or burnt grass, but the wind moving little spiral eddies of ash would soon blot them out. He stopped to sniff at a stinging burnt patch on his ribs, and realised that he was no silver horse at all, but drawn over with charcoal and dusted grey with the ash. He would not gleam silver against the black.

Every time he passed the remains of a dead animal he shied, but there were not many. He hoped that most of the animals had managed to save themselves by getting to the water. The fire had travelled so fast that wombats should be safe in their holes — but would wallabies and kangaroos get to water? What of horses? What of Storm?

Storm? Storm? Storm? His hoofs beat out the question.

He went more cautiously as he dropped down towards The Tin Mine Creek, and stopped amongst some gaunt, smouldering candlebarks to look along the valley. Great patches of the grass had not been burnt where it was green or boggy, and a few disconsolate horses stood near the water. A mob of kangaroos hopped restlessly from one green patch to another. Some wallabies nibbled the grass at the water's edge.

Steel, whose bimble this was, was nowhere to be seen.

Thowra stepped out of his poor shelter and walked towards

121

the other horses. The horses jumped with fright as they saw him coming. They were all still shaking when he stopped to talk to them.

"Greetings, on this grim morning," Thowra said. "I would have news if you can give me any. Where is Steel, or did the fire catch him? Where are the mares and foals of this herd?"

One well-grown, dun stallion answered.

"Greetings, O Silver Horse," he said. "We do not know because we were blown here on the wings of the great wind, blown in front of the fire," but he looked at a yearling who stood on three legs.

"I am of Steel's herd," the yearling was trembling with fear – not of Thowra but of the horror which had been. "My leg was hurt and I couldn't gallop. I fell into the creek and the red fire passed over me."

"You were lucky," said Thowra. "What of Steel?"

"I do not know. They all galloped in front of the wind and the flames." The young horse's head sank to the ground in misery.

"Steel would," Thowra said cheerfully. Then, feeling sorry for the yearling, he bumped him gently with his nose. "Be not downcast. I have not seen many dead animals in my travels. The herd will probably come back to plague you and eat the greenest grass before you can reach it on your lame leg."

He went off thinking: "Where there is water there is not death," but there were only the soaks on Stockwhip Gap, and the little trickling creeks that went down the valleys from the gap. What of Storm . . . Storm . . . Storm . . . ? What of his own son, Lightning, last seen in the dense bush going towards Quambat? What of Cirrus?

Thowra trotted on. He could only go one way at a time, and Baringa would look for Lightning and for Cirrus. He must go on to the Secret Valley as well as finding Storm. This was the way he must go.

Only some of the divide between the Tin Mine Creek and the Ingegoodbee had burnt, and, above the huts, the big trees were untouched. Thowra felt an intense relief to be in amongst living trees again. He went with care, because there was always the possibility of men where there were huts.

No smoke went up from the chimneys. There was no movement round the huts or yards, and where the valley widened and was threaded through by the meandering river quite a few brumbies were standing as though still afraid to graze. The hills on the other side were gaunt and black, and smoke hung over all the mountains he could see.

He must find Storm.

For a flashing moment he thought he saw him, and then realised that it was Son of Storm who was so like his sire. Without taking up time to go down into the valley to speak to him, Thowra turned to the north.

Soon he was going over a black burnt land again, his hoof-beats were deadened by the ash that rose swirling round his legs. More and more, as he trotted on, he was oppressed by the utter silence.

The bush had been thick here, with no stream close by. He shied violently from something below a fallen tree. Three horses had died there, and there were more charred bodies of horses and even of kangaroos as he got further into the bush.

Thowra began to sweat with horror. He broke into a canter, and the ash rose even higher around him.

Storm . . . Storm . . . Storm . . . He must find Storm.

The scrub had burnt right to the banks of the Moyangul. How could beast or bird survive? The mountain ash had burnt, the tea tree had burnt; higher up towards the Gap, snowgums had burnt. Thowra had to slow to a trot. His flanks were heaving. He must find Storm.

The fire had burnt fiercely in the thick bush towards the head of the Cascade Creek. Stockwhip Hill was still smoulder-ing and was black, black, black. The Lookout was burnt right to its pile up rocks, but he could see that the big old, gnarled snowgums on the gap were still standing, though the grass was blackened between them. Perhaps it had not been so very bad there. He went on and on, straining upwards faster and faster.

On the Gap there was no sign of life, no sound. Only the black silence. Thowra listened to this terrible silence and felt despair. Standing there in the black gap, among the drifting eddies of ash, the Silver Brumby raised his head in one long forlorn neigh:

"Brother of the wind and the storm where are you?"

Only the silence pressed in from all around.

Baringa went out before daybreak to learn if Lightning and

Cirrus had survived; and Cloud, also Goonda and her foal. More than anything, he wished to know the whereabouts of The Ugly One – charred flesh and bone or a living horse.

He had the two mares he wanted, safely in his deep, hidden canyon, but he knew that he was very unlikely to keep them if he took them out to wander wild and free all over the mountains. The Ugly One, if he were living, would assuredly come for Moon – and what of Lightning?

Baringa, not yet a three-year-old, possessor of the two most beautiful mares in the mountains, climbed out of his canyon, plagued with uncertainty about the two horses whom he sought – Lightning, his dam's full brother, who would never leave him in peace while he had Dawn and Moon, and the mad bay stallion who would surely kill him if he could, and whom Baringa himself must some day kill if he would own the silver fillies.

Smoke hid the stars still, and the air was deathly cold. When Baringa pulled himself up over the last rocks the darkness and the cold grew deeper, greater, and there was the smell of a burnt land rising round him with every step, bitter in his nostrils.

Everything was dark, sky and ground, and it was impossible to see even the outline of a fallen tree. Baringa felt his way along, knowing when something was ahead of him only by the feel of the air.

The valley was changed because many of the trees he knew and shrubs in which he had hidden were reduced to ash.

When daylight began to seep through the smoky air and the cold night, Baringa kept a very careful lookout, but he saw no living thing. Like Thowra, he shied away from the burnt animals that lay in the ash: like Thowra he was oppressed by the silence that hung all over the mountains as though nothing were alive.

Yet there were not many dead animals, and he had not seen one dead horse.

He went on and on towards Quambat. Cirrus should be there, and Lightning would most surely have headed there when he had first felt the choking fear of the smoke, but there was not much water at Quambat. Unless the horses had gone downstream, there were no waterholes big enough to hold even a foal – only the trickling stream that was sweet to drink.

There was no shadow horses flickering through the bush,

no kangaroos, no wallabies, no kurrawongs – no bush. Except for the patches of green grass here and there by the creek, all was black and so utterly silent.

Baringa found himself going slower because he was alone and afraid in all this empty, burnt-out land. As he got near the head of Dale's Creek he could see that the grass in the little hanging valley and round the soaks where the creek headed was unburnt.

Suddenly he stiffened and stopped in his tracks. Something had moved. Something was lying down, away up there ... something greyish ... (he crept along) ... or just covered in ash ... a horse? Surely The Ugly One would not be here, and he would make a darker heap ... (he crept closer) ... had it really moved, there on the patch of ash-covered grass ... (closer, closer) ... or was it dead?

The hairs of Baringa's coat were prickling with fear.

Yes, it moved ... a horse ... ? A pale horse ... ?

Baringa heard his own hooves as though they were thudding on hard-baked ground, not soundless in the ash. His heart was thudding against his ribs.

The horse raised its head, shook it, and then let it swing aimlessly from side to side.

The thudding of Baringa's heart was loud, shaking him.

It was Lightning! Why did he behave like that? Was he hurt?

Baringa still crept forward, wondering why Lightning took no notice, but in fact his movement was quite soundless.

Lightning was still lying there when Baringa had crept very close.

It was then that Baringa realised that Lightning's eyes were shut and watering. *He could not see.*

Baringa stopped, shocked. Then he nickered very softly.

"It is I, Baringa. What has befallen you?"

"Baringa!" Lightning said, rising unsteadily. "I cannot open my eyes."

Baringa came closer to him. There was no mark of burning on his head.

"Why are you here?" he asked.

"I galloped and galloped in front of the fire and then it caught me here and the bush was burning all around this grass for a long time. It was the smoke in my eyes and the ghastly heat. Now I cannot find my way back."

"If you follow close to me I will lead you to Quambat," Baringa said. "Tell me, did you see that ugly bay stallion galloping for his life?"

"No," Lightning replied. "Kangaroos and wallabies I saw, and wombats, rats, possums, dingos, but never a horse."

"Humph," Baringa muttered. "Now walk quietly, because I do not know what may be abroad."

"Nothing has come near me, and this must be the second day since the fire," Lightning said.

"Even so, we will take care. You would be unable to fight even a yearling."

There were still a few miles to go before they would see Quambat Flat. Lightning began to seem stronger as they walked, his shoulder against Baringa's flank.

All of a sudden Baringa propped and snorted.

"What is it?" Lightning asked sharply.

"A dead horse." Baringa's trembling went from him to Lightning, through their hair as they touched shoulder to flank. "The bush was thick, here," Baringa went on, "and this horse is burnt more than the other dead animals I have seen. I wonder who it was?"

"Many horses that we did not know lived here," Lightning said, his nostrils dilated. "Come away."

"I would like to know who it is," said Baringa, forcing himself closer.

Lightning, because he was afraid of losing contact with Baringa, unwillingly went too.

"Why," he asked, "are you so anxious to know where that mad bay stallion is? Is this just one dead horse alone?"

"This is one alone," answered Baringa, looking suspiciously at Lightning, and he did not add that the horse was burnt beyond recognition.

Even blind, Lightning would be thinking of the white fillies, and when Baringa looked closely at his eyes he felt fairly sure that they were only stuck together, and that Lightning would not be blind for ever.

Soon they were over the gap and dropping down through the burnt and smouldering forest towards the Quambat.

Several times they passed dead horses. Baringa did not mention them but Lightning knew, and asked if any were horses they knew.

Baringa looked round at him again.

126

"If you really rubbed your eyes they'd maybe open and you might see that you and I have been lucky."

"What do you mean, rub my eyes?"

"They look as if they are only stuck together. Rub 'em on your legs."

"It hurts." Lightning let out a squeal as he tried rubbing one open, but he could feel that the lids were indeed less tightly held together. He tried both eyes almost savagely and got them to open slightly.

"I can see a little," he said. "Blurry," but he was excited.

"Well, your eyes are in quite a mess. I should think they will be all right, though," Baringa said, and led on again till they were getting near Quambat, and he tried to find some cover in which to hide while he looked over the flat. There were a few smouldering trees and he hid behind them. Lightning was still keeping against him.

They looked out on eerie emptiness – the polished black of Quambat Flat.

"Not a horse," Baringa whispered.

"Isn't *anyone* there? I can't see."

"No one. We'll go down the edge of the flat, keeping in what trees there are."

Baringa moved on, thinking that where the creek had been joined by other streams they might find horses. Even with Lightning beside him – the sound of his breath, the slight sound of his footfalls – the silence that hung over Quambat Flat made him feel that something dreadful was still to come, not passed already.

There was so little cover in which to hide.

Then Baringa saw a few living trees at a bend in the creek, and among them he saw some horses standing with drooping heads – and in a flash he thought: "There is nothing to eat!"

He led Lightning quietly on.

It was Goonda who saw them first. She gave a glad little neigh and came trotting towards them, her foal at her heels.

With a sigh of relief, Baringa saw Cloud and Cirrus. That which he had promised to do for Thowra was done. He could go home now – if he could get away unfollowed.

He left Lightning with Goonda and went to Cirrus and Cloud.

"Greetings for my sire, the Silver Stallion," he said rather

127

gravely. "He is safe. He bade me see if you also had survived the fire."

"Greetings Baringa," Cirrus answered. "Is the Silver Stallion unhurt?"

"A few burns, just as I have a few burns," Baringa answered. "How did you find safety when the bush blazed?"

"In the creek, on bare ground, and who knows how? Some of us found we were still alive when we thought we were dead."

Baringa noted some strangers in the group and thought that all horses must be brothers because of the fire. Presently, when the others were no longer gathered around him, he asked Cirrus if an ugly, slab-shouldered bay stallion had been seen galloping from the fire.

The Ugly One had not been to Quambat.

After a while Baringa slipped quietly away, heading for the high plateau, but intending to go up as nearly as possible over the same ground as The Ugly One must have galloped down in front of the fire. All the way up he searched for the burnt remains of a horse and it was late afternoon by the time he reached the plateau at about the place where he had last seen The Ugly One and from where he had taken Moon. An uneasy wind stirred the ash on the ground. Gaunt trees held black and leafless branches to the windy sky.

Baringa, having found nothing on the way up, thought that if The Ugly One were living he would probably come back to see if his Hidden Filly yet lived.

There was no hoofmark nor droppings. Living or dead, The Ugly One had left no sign.

To the Death

So the wind over the black bush whispered: "Where, where, where?"

Thowra sought Storm, and Baringa climbed out of his canyon seeking The Ugly One, night after night.

There was another question which filled the whole being of every animal, which seemed part of the earth itself: "Rain? When will it rain? When will there be grass?"

While there was no grass out in the mountains, Baringa's fillies and Koora and the kangaroos were quite contented to

128

stay in the Canyon where there was still some grazing. They were sleeker than the other animals who had had to live on the patches of grass around creek heads and the leaves which the deep-rooting shrubs had put out.

Day after day the sun blazed down through dry air: night after night the stars blazed ice-cold and the cold wind blew, blowing the ash and the charcoal, freezing the unfed horses to the bone.

But, even on the blackened trunks of the eucalypts, soft green leaves grew as the trees were forced to replace their burnt leaves so that they might breathe and also use the energy of the burning sun – so that they might live.

Then at last clouds rolled up over the sky and there came a night when every animal knew it was going to rain.

Baringa was too restless to stay in the Canyon, and as the heavy evening closed in, he went up the cliff once more, on to the high plateau, and searched and searched in case The Ugly One had returned. While he was there the rain began to come down in great drops, splashing the ash up around his legs, and soon running in black rivulets along the cracks in charcoaled logs.

While the ground grew wetter Baringa danced and bucked and then rolled joyously as his coat felt damp and loose.

For days he had been beginning to think that The Ugly One must be dead, and now, in a great rush of well-being, he felt sure that the mad bay would have returned by now if he were alive.

The rain began to fall more steadily. Baringa started back towards the Canyon, while the ash and dust and charcoal turned to mud under his hooves. The tracks that he could not avoid making would be washed out quite soon.

He reached the cliff and jumped down on to the first shelf, then slowly picked his way downwards. By the time he reached the bottom, the rain had eased off. In the morning the sun shone again, but the animals all knew that more rain was coming.

Lazy clouds drifted across the sky all morning. By afternoon the sky was covered with heavy grey and black clouds. The air was hot and breathless. The whole land, the few birds who had returned, and the beasts were all waiting.

Koora moved restlessly, as restlessly as a wind blows. Thowra must return some day.

Baringa and his two lovely fillies were tense, excited.

The clouds grew heavier. A kurrawong cried wildly up above the cliff. Baringa looked up in the direction of the far-away cry, up, up at the cliff which he had climbed so often.

Then something seemed to stop inside him. For a moment he himself was only made of fear, or of horror: then his heart began to thud inside his ribs, sweat broke out on his silver hide – behind his ears, down his neck, down his quarters.

On the edge of the cliff stood a horse.

Baringa seemed turned to quartz. He stood absolutely still head up, watching while the horse jumped down on to the first shelf, and saw it sniff at the ground.

Then Baringa knew what had given his secret away. The rain, last night, had stopped too soon to wash out his tracks. The Ugly One had been able to follow them, and his hoof-mark, deeply indented where he landed on the shelf, baked hard into last night's mud, had been the final clue.

The bay horse on the cliff looked down at him and then gave a mad, wild neigh that echoed round and round the Canyon – and started down.

Baringa stood for a few moments, so horrified that he could not move. He had been wrong, for The Ugly One still lived. At last he told his mares to start up the opposite canyon wall, and asked Benni, if he were killed, to take them to Son of Storm. Then he moved across the creek where he could no longer be seen from above, and started up the cliff, slightly upstream from the usual way – and Baringa knew the cliff well.

Benni made the two silver mares and Koora and Dilkara climb very fast. He was determined to reach a place from which they would get a flying start to escape and yet where they could watch.

"Baringa must fight to kill – or be killed – before he is a full-grown horse," Benni said, and he sounded anxious. "Come," he added. "If The Ugly One wins, you must get right away," and he looked at Moon, wondering what she wished. He saw that she was terrified. Later, when they stopped, high up on the steep wall, so that they could see what was going on, he saw how desperately she was torn between her anxiety to watch Baringa and her anxiety to escape from The Ugly One. He touched her nose with his soft paw:

"Don't be too afraid," he whispered. "Baringa will, I think, one day be king of the horses of the south, just as Thowra became king of the Cascade brumbies." Then he added: Thowra defeated a bigger, stronger horse, one named Arrow, in a way of which I think Baringa may have heard ..." But Benni was really very worried. This fight was coming too early in Baringa's life.

They saw Baringa climbing up the cliff and realised that neither of the horses could see each other. The Ugly One was climbing down so fast that he sent a shower of stones with almost every step.

Benni knew that Baringa had been all over this cliff many times; he watched him now, springing carefully from rock to rock.

"He knows just where he wants to get him," thought Benni. "It is a desperate chance, but if he had waited till he got down, and fought him on the canyon floor, then The Ugly One would almost undoubtedly have won."

Baringa was hanging on with his neat, hard hooves and edging across the cliff.

Benni gave a deep sigh. The white moth was too high on the cliff, too far above The Ugly One.

Sweat was pouring off the two mares. They were both still gasping for breath after their steep climb under the hot, heavy clouds, and now they were afraid – but they watched Baringa, light as a moth, fly down the cliff. The Ugly One was making so much noise himself that he could not have heard the sudden flight from above, for he never looked up.

"*Now*," said Benni. "Yet how can he cause The Ugly One to fall and not crash down himself?" And the mares were standing shaking beside him.

Baringa paused on the cliff, straight above The Ugly One, and then deliberately kicked a small rock down.

The rock hit a jutting-out piece of the cliff and flew clear of the bay, whizzing past his head.

Baringa kicked another one just as he looked up. This time the rock landed on the bay's rump, cutting a gash.

The Ugly One screamed.

Baringa slid from one shelf to another, sending a cascade of stones down on the other horse.

Benni sat straight up.

"He may win by driving the other horse mad till it falls," he said.

"He *is* mad," whispered Moon, "and cruel." She was

131

trembling with terror, her eyes fastened on the young silver stallion and the heavy bay on the opposite cliff, and sometimes the clouds seemed to creep into the Canyon so that it was difficult to see – or was it her own sweat and fear that blurred her vision? For the last few weeks she had been happier than she had ever been.

Baringa was closer to The Ugly One, still showering him with stones. The bay tried going even faster down the cliff. Baringa bounded after him and more rocks came thudding down.

The bay stumbled and nearly fell, but Baringa was desperate too. Somehow he must kill the bay stallion before he could cross the creek.

There was a long sloping shelf that led right to the edge of the great landslide beside the cliff. The usual way down was to go half-way along this shelf and twist back on to an outcrop of rocks running the opposite way.

This shelf would give Baringa his chance, if only he had maddened The Ugly One enough.

As The Ugly One reached the shelf and started hurrying along it, Baringa leapt down and landed on the shelf behind him.

"Now," said Benni. "Now!"

Baringa sprang at the hastening rump, and bit hard, then struck and slashed as the other wheeled.

Benni stiffened into a grey statue. Baringa must fight to kill and yet not crash down the cliff himself. The bay was mad enough not to care if they crashed to their death together so long as he killed Baringa.

Baringa had the advantage of being the highest up on the sloping shelf. He used this advantage in a leaping, thunderous attack.

The bay backed and lost more height. Baringa sprang for him again. This time the big bay stood firm and was ready to drive back, but Baringa, quick as light, leapt upwards on to a jutting rock.

Down came a slab on the bay's head, and Baringa followed it, slashing furiously, but always pressing himself against the cliffside.

The Ugly One stepped back again.

"Now, now," thought Baringa, leaping back to avoid a great,

striking hoof, and then leaping forward again to slash at the bay head.

The Ugly One was already past the place where he should have left the shelf.

"Now!" thought Baringa. "This is the time. Now I must win!" He whirled in again, but The Ugly One met him chest on, with a terrific impact.

Baringa recoiled but was jumping forward again before the heavier horse could move. He felt his hoof strike through flesh to bone. The bay kept coming.

"If I don't force him back on to that landslide he will kill me!" Baringa knew it – knew it from the tips of his ears to his hard hooves. He pushed his rump back into the cliff and then sprang again, using teeth and feet.

The Ugly One's teeth only just slipped off his own wither.

Baringa felt the sweat run faster and then turn cold. If the bigger horse got a grip it might be the end.

The bay let out one of his insane screams. There was a little bump of rock only a foot above the shelf; Baringa took one jump on to it and then off it on to the great slabby shoulder.

A tremor went through Benni as he wondered if Baringa was getting too desperate and would blunder.

Baringa crashed both forefeet into the other horse, felt the cliff behind him, then sunk his teeth into The Ugly One's withers. Then he began to push him back along the shelf and also towards the edge.

The sweat was pouring down him and he knew he would not have the strength to hold the heavier horse for long, but if he could damage him . . . if he could frighten him . . . if he could force him yet further back . . . force him on to that landslide. . . . Baringa hung on and braced himself against the cliff, pressing his quarters into it, pushing pushing, for he must live and The Ugly One must die.

The Ugly One struggled and struggled, screamed and screamed.

Baringa's grip began to slip, his jaws were aching. He felt the sweat pouring down his flanks, running round his eyes, down his neck. The Ugly One would shake him off soon and then, when he felt himself going, he must leap back, and quickly up above him again – and attack.

Benni and the mares stood still, so still, watching the two stallions struggling – Baringa, the streak of light, and the bay,

133

more difficult to pick out from the cliff. Already it was getting late, and the rain clouds were becoming heavier and heavier. Dilkara found a rock against which he could lie, and went to sleep.

On the cliff the two stallions still battled. Suddenly they were apart, Baringa leapt above, and was showering the stones down again. Benni could see he was tired.

The Ugly One backed out of range of the flying stones and in a second Baringa had jumped down, struck him, and leapt back. More stones came down.

The landslide which was an immense scree – a wide strip of loose rock and stone, stretching right down to the creek – was not far behind the bay.

Baringa jumped, striking blow after blow at his head – then up he went again, then down, striking, leaping, dancing. Gradually he drove The Ugly One back, but he, himself, was nearing exhaustion.

The Ugly One now tried to attack. Baringa sprang nimbly out of the way and kicked another rock down. This happened several times and then Baringa charged in again, a little rested, perhaps a little more desperate.

Benni's forepaws came higher, nearer his face as he saw the two horses locked together, wavering on the edge of the shelf.

"The mad one will pull him over," whispered Dawn, but Baringa managed to jump back on to his cliff again and fight himself free.

Then he seemed to dance out in the most desperate piece of daring. He leapt up above the shelf on to a narrow rib of rock, and danced and mocked the older horse. From there he landed behind the bay, struck and kicked – and lured him round towards the landslide.

Before The Ugly One could catch him, Baringa was just out of reach, above the shelf, but very close to the scree. The big horse tried to jump up, failed, and landed badly, though still on the shelf.

Baringa was down in a flash.

The big horse was off balance. Baringa drove at him so hard that he stepped back. Rearing up, Baringa struck again.

There was a sudden sound of scrabbling hooves and sliding stones.

The Ugly One's hind feet were on the scree.

Quick!

Baringa with bursting lungs, rushed at him, pushing, shoving. The Ugly One fought for a foothold.

Benni and the mares could hear the rattle of the sliding stones from the opposite side.

"The light is going," whispered Benni, but just then the scree began to move under the bay's hind legs, and he was going too, amongst a mass of moving stones.

"Baringa has won," Benni said.

Seeking Storm

The rain poured over the mountains. Dale's Creek, in flood, washed logs and branches and even the body of a horse out of the Canyon.

The Creek came out over Quambat Flat. The Ingegoodbee was in full spate, the Moyangul and the Tin Mine Creek. Charcoal Creek was flooding, and half a hundred little rivulets filled the Cascade Creek to overflowing. The stream that ran through the Secret Valley roared over its rocks.

Through all the mountains which had been silent, there was now the sound of rushing water. And when the rain was done and the hot sun came out, there was the carolling of magpies, the pipe of the white-throated tree-creepers, the lovely song of Harmonica, the grey thrush.

A mist of green crept over the whole land and then there were leaves and the first faint needles of snowgrass.

Thowra knew that now, if Storm yet lived, he should return. Once more he went seeking.

The fire had not burnt as far up into the mountains as Dead Horse Gap and the Crackenback River, nor was Paddy Rush's Bogong or The Brindle Bull burnt, though a lot of the bush above the Cascades had gone.

There were some horses that had been in Storm's herd in the Cascades, but they had seen nothing of Storm. He went on. Surely he would find him on Stockwhip Gap.

Even though he was wondering about Storm, he could not help feeling joy in the springy, damp earth, in the warm, wet scent – could not help feeling the same up-springing strength of growth and rebirth himself. The world was renewed, and he danced along on light hooves.

There had been horses on Stockwhip Gap because he saw their tracks, but there was no track of Storm or of any of his well-known mares.

At last he turned down into the valley where he had first seen old Whiteface, first seen Koora – and there, lurking in the burnt trees, was Whiteface himself.

Thowra went down with his swinging, proud walk, and struck an attitude in front of him.

"Cunning enough to get away from the fire!" he said cheerfully, "and I see that you've not gone hungry since. Where have you been?"

Whiteface looked both deaf and surly.

"Come now!" said Thowra. "None of your tricks. Answer my friendly question. You know what happens if you don't! Where have you been?"

"Suggan Buggan," Whiteface answered primly.

Thowra's ears flickered slightly, then he walked around the herd, still wondering if the cunning old fox had fooled him. He saw a rather handsome mare and decided to ask her if she had seen any sign of Storm.

"He wasn't over Suggan Buggan way," she answered.

"So you really were there!"

The mare looked surprised.

"We swung that way escaping from the fire," she replied.

Thowra had searched and searched for Storm and did not know where to search next. He wandered rather slowly towards the Ingegoodbee. It was when he was near the head of the river that he saw the emus.

The great birds were walking slowly towards him, their feathers bouncing.

"They told me of that hollow in the ground, and of the silver bird," Thowra thought. "Perhaps they will tell me where I can find my brother, Storm." So he grazed along, waiting till the birds came right up to him. Then he looked up, his proud eyes meeting their fierce ones.

"Greetings, O emus," he said.

"Greetings, Silver Stallion," they replied.

"Since the fire, O noble birds, I have not found my brother, Storm. Have you seen or heard of him?"

"Surely," said the male emu, "it might be more interesting to contemplate the actions of your son at present."

"Oh?" Thowra waited.

"Yes. You should hurry to the Tin Mine Creek crossing on The Pilot track," the emu continued. "Sometimes we, with our high heads and sharp eyes, can see the future . . ."

("Or imagine you can," thought Thowra.)

". . . . but you have created a situation in the south – leaving your son and grandson there – the outcome of which we cannot see."

"Oh?" Thowra murmured again, beginning to wonder if Lightning and Baringa were fighting.

"But of course this was Steel's fault," the emu announced after a little silent thought. "He was the aggressor."

"Ah, Steel was? He is an aggressive type."

"Yes, yes," said the emu, suddenly speaking much quicker. "We will come with you. We were only saying, as we came along, that we should have waited to see who was the victor."

Thowra found himself cantering along with the two long-striding emus stepping it out beside him.

"If I have never looked funny before, I must certainly look funny now," Thowra thought, casting a sidelong glance at his strange companions.

"Tell me," he said, as he cantered. "What was Steel's fault?"

"Oh, Lightning was out on one of his wanderings – searching for Baringa and his beautiful filly, I should think . . ."

Thowra realised that there was *one* thing the emus did not know. They did not know that Baringa had two fillies.

". . . . and Steel saw him. He came roaring down to Lightning, telling him to go back to the Cascades or he would murder him. He may have murdered him . . . but he was the thinner of the two . . . Too little feed."

The emu's mate spoke for the first time:

"Lightning will beat Steel," she said, "and then Lightning will imagine himself king, because both Cloud and Son of Storm are peaceable horses, and there are no other stallions of any great importance." With that she said no more, and Thowra thought she had said enough anyway.

They could hear the fight from half a mile away, but from the screams of triumph, they knew it was ending. When they

137

got close, Lightning was putting in his last few blows.

They stopped to watch. The emus said nothing.

Steel sank to the ground. Lightning gave him a parting kick, and went proudly seeking Steel's mares who had started to slide away.

"Ha!" said Thowra aloud. "He has learnt some sense. He's not trying to round up the lot, he's going for those two good looking light greys."

The female emu spoke for the second time:

"He, too, would build a silver herd." And once again she had said enough. For there was Lightning, triumphant, lording it over the vanquished horse's mares, choosing the light greys who were almost silver like himself, though doubtless the one whom he had really been seeking, when he left the Quambat, was Baringa's Dawn, and perhaps the dream vision of the Hidden Filly.

Thowra turned away, followed by the emus. Presently, he said:

"Well now, what can you tell me of Storm?"

"He lives," the emu replied, "but he has moved from where we last saw him, probably searching for grass. One reason why he did not return straight away, is that the oldest of his mares was lamed by a falling tree, during the gallop from the fire, and he would not leave her. Anyway there was no food," the emu eyed Thowra's sleek, well-fed-looking coat.

"You will see him before the winter comes – and it will come soon," the emu's mate said.

"This will be a very heavy winter," announced the emu, himself. "Snow will come early and there will be a lot of it. You may not see us again till the spring."

It was not till night-time that Lightning started to move, wih his two new mares, towards Quambat. They went along slowly through the darkness, and off the track into Dale's Creek, seeking good grazing. There they wandered carelessly up the stream, drinking the reflected stars, eating the short, sweet grass.

Lightning had fought a big fight and he was tired and stiffening a little, but he was very pleased with himself, and went proudly.

A moon rose late, throwing a faint light. The landscape

was charcoal and silver. Suddenly Lightning stood transfixed. Were there three phantom silver horses — a young, lithe stallion and two mares? Was it one mare? Or were they phantoms of his imagination? Was there only one silver stallion?

He leapt forward — past the stallion, who was undoubtedly real — and madly, furiously after the mares, who had perhaps never really been there at all.

Then something came through the air and hit him with terrific impact on the off shoulder. He was knocked off balance. In a moment Baringa was dancing in front of him.

Lightning tried to brush Baringa out of the way, but Baringa charged him again and once more knocked him off balance. This time Lightning, the victor over Steel, came after him to strike him hard enough to make him behave himself and leave his elders alone!

Baringa dodged, almost knocked Lightning over, and was out of reach in a flash.

"Did I not lead you, Lightning, when you were blind from the smoke?" he said scornfully.

Really angry now, Lightning reared, screaming, and then leapt at Baringa.

Baringa twisted away, tapped Lightning maddeningly on the nose with one hoof, and was round behind him. Dancing, striking, always keeping out of reach — an infuriating silver streak — Baringa led Lightning away from the direction in which the mares had gone.

He saw the pale grey mares and recognised them as part of Steel's herd. Soon the fact that Lightning was already nearing exhaustion and that he had these mares with him, fitted into a picture.

"You have fought Steel today," Baringa said in a jeering tone, because he wanted an answer, and he gave Lightning a stinging kick.

"Fought Steel!" Lightning exclaimed with fury. "I've thrashed him!" His breath was coming in gasps, but he had to add: "I have the pick of his young mares."

Baringa might have thought what a joke it would be to exhaust Lightning and steal the mares, but they were so plain compared with his lovely ones, and all his mind was taken up with how he could be finished with Lightning and then track Dawn and Moon till he joined them, and take them back to safety in his secret canyon.

Lightning was very tired. He, too, wished he could finish off this fight. Not really thinking to hurt Baringa: certainly forgetting Thowra's command, he struck fiercely at him.

Baringa moved so quickly that it was only a glancing blow, but it cut him and he knew that Lightning, his dam's full brother, had really struck him.

He flung himself at Lightning and knocked him off balance, then again, and this time knocked him over.

Lightning staggered to his feet. Baringa knocked him over again – and then Baringa was no longer there. He had melted away in amongst the shadows, the moonlight, and the charcoaled trees.

When Lightning asked the mares which way he had gone, they said towards The Pilot, but very soon Baringa had swung back, was nosing around to pick up any sign Dawn and Moon had left, and was tracking them, though they had gone like ghosts, up on to the high plateau. There he found them and led them down the cliff to join Koora and her foal and the two kangaroos.

"What happened?" asked Benni, seeing the blood running from a deep cut under Baringa's mane.

"Lightning," answered Baringa. "Once I saved him from that Steel whom he has beaten today, and I led him to Quambat when he was blind, but there is no safety for Dawn and Moon until I am strong enough for Lightning to know I am master, and that these silver mares are mine."

The All-smothering Snow

The emus were right, Thowra thought. The snow was coming early, and as he saw the big flakes drifting down from the evening sky above the Secret Valley, he remembered the time he had stood on The Lookout Platform and seen Storm twisted and whirled upwards like an ascending geni, by the willy willies of snow.

Filled with snow restlessness now, he went up the cliff path to The Lookout Platform. The longer he stood there, with the flakes falling cold on rump, back and withers, and matting in mane and forelock, the more he thought of Storm, till at last he turned and went up the cliff, over the edge by the scrub

140

bush, and out among the ghostly ribbon-gums and candlebarks. Then he set off at the trot towards the south.

The snow collected on his eyelashes, it lay on his coat. He felt that same old excitement which had come with the first snowfall of every winter since he was a foal running at Bel Bel's side. He remembered getting a nip from Bel Bel for leaping on to a rock and neighing because he was excited: he remembered the fights: he remembered what a hard winter it was. This winter might be worse, with even less food.

Thowra found himself in the old familiar country, trotting on and on through the curtain of snow. The tracks were invisible, but they were the tracks he and Storm had followed together in many other snowstorms.

This was the way they had come when they were first on their own. Along this track they had brought their first mares. Storm was like a ghost beside him, so strongly was he in his mind.

On Thowra went, alone, through the falling snow. At last he was turning down Yarraman's Valley. It was here that he and Storm had become grown horses, having to fend for themselves because Yarraman, their sire, was dead.

He climbed on to the rock from which he had looked down on the great dead chestnut horse – and was sure he saw a dark shape of a horse moving through the snow down in the valley.

He stood perfectly still. It might be imagination. Yet there it was again. He was there. He, too, might be seeking the old tracks and the old ways on this first night of snow. And Thowra neighed softly.

"Storm, brother of the wild wind, here am I."

From below came the answer:

"Hail! O my brother!" and Storm came leaping up on to the rock to join him.

They reared: they nipped each other. They rubbed their heads together, and the cold snow falling on them, melted where their heads touched.

"I have sought you ever since the fire, brother," said Thowra, touching him on the wither with his nose.

"I could not return earlier," Storm answered, "because my brown mare, Kalari, full sister to your Boon Boon, was badly lamed, and I could not leave her."

"So the emus spoke the truth," Thowra said. "Is Kalari all right?" He remembered how he and Storm had first got them-

141

selves small herds, their mares being daughters of The Brolga. Among his was the faithful, wise Boon Boon. Storm's Kalari was a wise, good mare too.

"No," Storm answered sadly, "and we have travelled very slowly because of her. We are here in the Cascades – just some of us. She wanted her old home."

"I see," said Thowra, head up to the falling snow. "This snow will not last, but the emus, who seem to speak truth, say it will be a very heavy winter."

"I feel it will be, myself," said Storm, and added, "Kalari wanted to come here so much."

Thowra thought how Kalari was older than Boon Boon and had had many foals, and he wondered if the snow would indeed stop and melt away before the real winter started – but now, for a night, he and Storm could wander through their own country once more made strange by the slow-drifting flakes.

They crossed the Cascade Creek and went up past the cattlemen's hut and through the twisted snowgums, up over the top of the ridge and then down, down through the whispering corridors between the great, tall mountain ash. A very old wombat was grubbing furiously for grass and roots. He looked up as they came along.

"Ah, Silver Horse," he said. "Many snows have gone by since you were here, but I knew you would return, you and your noble brother. Take heed for there is going to be heavy, heavy snow."

The silence was only broken by the sighing of the streamers of bark on the high trees. Then Storm lowered his nose down to the wombat.

"Venerable wombat," he said, "will this snow that is falling now be deep and remain until the spring?"

"Who am I to know?" answered the wombat, "but for horses who cannot live when snow covers the ground very deeply, I think it is time to be gone."

"And I have only succeeded in getting Kalari here two days ago," said Storm.

Back in the Secret Valley the snow had barely lain at all, but not many days went past before the sky became closed in – grey, heavy – and Thowra knew that snow would fall again.

142

What he did not know was that it had never melted off the higher country. Then that evening, when the flakes were already filling the sky, Thowra looked up, and there, on The Lookout Platform, was a movement – the shape of a horse made misty behind the veil of falling snow!

Storm!

Thowra went swiftly up the cliff path.

"Greetings, my brother," said Storm. "My tracks are already covered, and for the safety of your secret, I have come by the Hidden Valley."

"The cliffs must have been slippery?"

"They were," said Storm who had enjoyed being poised in space with a snowstorm hiding him from the world. "I have come, not for help, but, I think, for your company for an hour or so."

"You are in trouble?" Thowra asked.

"The snow never melted, and now it comes to stay, I'm sure, and Kalari will not leave the Cascades."

Thowra put his head up to the touch of the cold flakes. Had not Bel Bel, his mother, said that her bones should bleach on the Ramshead? Kalari was born in the Cascades, and there she had lived out most of her life.

"Perhaps it is thus that she wishes it," he said. "She was badly hurt."

"Yes," said Storm sadly, "but what of the herd? The herd may have to go Suggan Buggan way, or low down on the Ingeegoodbee. And if I leave her – how lonely!"

"How lonely," thought Thowra, but that was how Bel Bel had wanted it.

Baringa watched the snow falling in his canyon. It did not fall thickly, nor lie much on the ground, because the Canyon was low and warm. As usual he was filled with restlessness at the start of a snowfall.

The kangaroos, who had been away, were back again and very uneasy.

Baringa found Benni standing beside him at the lower end of the Canyon.

"What is it, Benni?" he asked.

"I don't like it," the kangaroo answered. "I think there is going to be immense snow. We could all be trapped here."

143

"And if I take my mares out of the Canyon, Lightning will try to steal them," said Baringa. "I would love to take them out to race with the wind and roll in the snow, but it is not safe, not until I am strong enough to be able to beat Lightning – and he knows it. Perhaps he might be friendly again then. I do not want to hurt him."

Benni looked very thoughtful. Then he said:

"I don't think Lightning will be worrying about stealing fillies soon, nor will you be wanting to roll in the snow and race with the wind. There will be too much snow altogether."

"Here it is low," said Baringa.

"Yes, it is low," Benni answered, "but it is completely surrounded by much higher country," and he sighed, for something was telling him that they should go even lower. "If we could get through the gorge to where this creek joins the Tin Mine Creek, and then go towards the sunset, down to the big river, we would be safe," he said.

"I will try to find a way, if you like."

"It would need to be a low-level track, because there will be more snow higher up," said Benni, "and *not* through water . . ." he tapped Baringa on the nose.

Snow continued to fall, but it did not lie on the floor of the Secret Valley nor on the floor of Baringa's canyon. Quambat Flat was bare in patches.

Cloud had told Lightning that he thought that if much snow started to fall again, he and his mares would make down the creek.

"It is time," Cloud said, as he stood beside a deep drift of snow, "that you looked after your sister's son and his young mare, instead of trying to take his mare for yourself. I think that this coming winter may mean death for many of us, and I fear for Baringa. You have made it impossible for him to run here, and I would that I knew where he is."

Heavy snow fell at the higher levels, and neither Thowra nor Baringa knew that this was so, though Thowra, having lived through many more winters, thought it might be happening.

He looked around his Secret Valley at his herd – knowing that he was going to leave again and might not easily get back. Kunama, with one chestnut foal at foot and in foal again, was, at least for the time, happy to stay quiet. Her experience of a hunted life had been too grim. Golden had become heavier.

She was still lovely, but it was to Boon Boon that he turned now.

"You will all be safe here," he told her. "I go to see how Storm and Kalari fare, and to make sure Baringa is all right."

It was a lowering evening, with snow just starting to fall, when Thowra approached the Cascades. He had had to plough through a lot of snow to get there, so he was not really surprised to see how much snow there was in the valley – not surprised, but definitely disquieted.

He could see no tracks, the white surface was unbroken. Perhaps Storm had persuaded Kalari to leave before the snow got too heavy. Perhaps Kalari had died. Perhaps . . . perhaps . . . . but how could he tell? And he felt uneasy.

He went on, sinking into the snow, on and on towards the top of the Cascade Valley where Kalari had been grazing when he met Storm on Yarraman's rock. The only sound was the cry of the wind higher up.

Then suddenly, through the waiting silence of the snow-storm, there came a neigh.

The cry was forlorn, lost, just a cry to the snow and to the mountains, and perhaps to Time that had been – and surely it was Storm who cried aloud in the lonely mountains.

So strange was the neigh that Thowra stayed silent, almost afraid of all that Storm might be calling up, for it was as though Yarraman might answer him, or Mirri, or Bel Bel – as though even Arrow might appear out of the falling snow, and Darkie, his dam, and they themselves be yearlings again, racing through the snowy night with joy.

Then the strange sensation – the sensation that those other horses who had enjoyed life here in these hills were just beyond the curtain of falling snow, waiting for one more such neigh to call them – faded away, and Thowra, himself, called:

"Storm! Storm! My brother, is that you?"

"Thowra! It is I."

"I am coming," Thowra neighed, and went plunging through the snow, sending up clouds of snow as he cantered up the valley.

He was tired long before he was near Storm, but something about that desperate cry of Storm's made him wish to hurry.

Everything would be all right if Storm came to meet him. Once they were together again and racing through the snow to beat the winter, to reach Baringa, to get to Quambat, those horses of the past would not haunt him and lurk just beyond the snowfall. Instead of expecting to see Bel Bel and hear Yarraman's great call, he would be thinking of Koora, Cirrus, Baringa, Lightning, and of all the unknown country that yet lay ahead.

Storm did not come to meet him. Thowra hurried on. At last he saw him standing under a tree very close to where The Brolga's herd had been grazing the day he and Storm chose their first mares. Kalari was lying on the ground beside him. He saw Storm drop his head as though he were telling her that he had come. The brown mare half raised her head and then gave a great sigh and her head dropped back on the snow, for she was dead.

Storm touched her with his nose.

"Come," said Thowra after a long silence. "It is time we went. She wished to end here, and now she has her wish. It is not going to be easy to get away through the snow. Where are the herd?"

"Working their way down Charcoal Creek. I started them off and then came back four or five days ago. It was hard to get over the Gap then, and much snow has fallen since." He looked back at Kalari.

"Come away," said Thowra. "Come with me to see if Baringa and Lightning are all right. We'll go by way of the mountain ash on the sunset-facing slopes."

A wind had started to blow in great blasts. The snow was pelting down and being blown into drifts. Thowra's deep tracks up the valley were filling already with the smothering snow.

When Storm looked back at Kalari once more, she was already covered.

Snow poured down all night long. The air was so thick that even to breathe was difficult. The wind howled.

The two horses floundered through drifts on the valley floor, struggled up past the snow-covered hut, and then between the laden trees, struggling onwards up to the tumbled-down horse yards where they must turn down into the mountain ash. Both horses knew that they were fighting for their lives now – knew that this all-smothering snow might make of them just a mound, as it had of Kalari.

The emus had certainly known. This winter was going to be a very heavy one.

146

Before he got too tired to think of anything but his own survival, Thowra realised that the snow was coming from the south-west, an unusual direction, and that his Secret Valley might still not be covered too deeply. The great snowfall might be mainly on this south-western area of the mountains, Quambat, Dale's Creek, the Tin Mine, the Cascades, and on the Range itself.

Gradually he and Storm got slower and slower, leaning their great chests against the wind, plodding on and on through the deep, soft, snow.

It was Benni who made Baringa really worried, but the Canyon was already filling with snow.

"We must go down to the big river," he said.

"Dawn is already heavy with foal," said Baringa, "and the way to the Tin Mine Creek is all but impossible."

"She must eat or die," Benni answered. "You lead and I will come last. We must start now, before even another paw's depth of snow falls."

"Come!" Baringa called his mares and Koora, as the kangaroo's desperation flashed through him too. Benni could feel the weather that was coming even better than he could. "We must go," he told the mares. "Benni knows that this snowfall is going to be tremendous."

Little Dilkara turned his face up to the flakes that dropped steadily into the Canyon and watched them without understanding.

Koora looked around the Canyon. Thowra had left her here, and here she should stay.

"I must wait here for Thowra," she said.

"He will find only your bones bleached by snow and wind," Silky said. "Baringa is in charge of you while Thowra is not here. You must stay alive, and to live you must go lower down."

So Baringa led along the knife-edge track he had found – the narrow toe-holds made perilous by a coating of snow. Dawn followed close on his heels, almost touching him because she was so afraid of the way he became invisible in the swift-falling snow, and behind her came Moon, close as possible too. Koora followed, nose to Moon's tail, with Dilkara's nose touching her hocks. Koora and the kangaroos were the only ones in the procession that showed up, and when they rounded a corner,

147

and the snow became wide-flung white pellets, even they were hard to see.

Baringa, the leader, got the full force of the wind. He wavered for a moment in the blast, and then hung on. Now he could not see ahead. He had been over these cliffs once before and he knew he must just go on. He strained his senses to find the way and yet to keep in communication with the mares who followed, and with Benni. If he flickered his ears backwards, he could tell they were all there, a wind-strung line of horses following him and believing in him. The way forward he knew, not by sight nor sound, but by some other sense that belonged to every part of his body, every hair of his coat.

As they went on he had to kick the snow off his footholds because, even on the cliffs, it was becoming deep wherever it could lie – deep and treacherous.

He would scrape with a hard front hoof until he could feel the good rock beneath, then scrape a hold with his other fore-foot. Slowly, slowly, the line of horses crept around the cliff. Baringa strained every sense, so that he would know the way. It was almost as though – joining himself with his whole world – he drew strength and understanding from the land itself and the air and the blizzard. One foot after the other, neither too high on the cliff, nor too low, he felt his way through the snow.

At last they were above the junction with the Tin Mine Creek.

Baringa looked up into invisibility, took a deep breath, drawing snow into his nostrils, and then he breathed out, as though trying to expel fear. The snow fell so thickly, beat so hard on the wind, that, even sheltered by cliffs as they were, Baringa knew without doubt that Benni was right. This menacing blizzard could bring death.

He started to pick his way slowly down, for here they must cross over. Benni would have to get wet!

Benni knew, of course, that it was inevitable. He looked with distaste at the swirling grey water with the snow falling into it – the thousands of white flakes striking the water and vanishing, but with more and more flakes to take their places.

Then the procession was across, and going on and on through the snow-thick air, and though they dropped lower as they went down the gorge of the Tin Mine Creek, the snow continued to fall thickly, blanketing rock and tree, filling crevices so that they stumbled over and over again and almost fell.

Baringa would look back in fear if he heard, through the silencing, stifling snow, anything that sounded like a horse falling.

They struggled on – the strung-out line of horses, fighting for their lives.

They were already lower than Baringa had expected snow to fall. By now he should have had his tired mares and the exhausted foal safely beyond the snow, but though they kept on, and the cliffs gave way to easier country, it seemed that the snow only became deeper and deeper.

Koora was now having to urge on her foal.

"We must stop for a little while and let him drink," she said at last, but while they stood, and the silver foal, with heaving flanks and trembling legs tried to suck, the air became even denser with falling flakes, and the snow piled up and up on the ground.

"You were right, Benni," said Baringa. "This is tremendous snow."

Benni's face was troubled.

"I think there may be snow almost to the river, but there it will not lie for very long and we will be able to live."

"If we get there," Baringa muttered.

"We will get there," said Benni.

The snow continued to fall, steadily, steadily – deep, silent, soft, so deep. Even down by the big river everything was buried in snow.

Late, in the darkness that first night of the heavy snowfall, a ghost mob of horses waded and ploughed their way down on to the river banks, too tired even to scratch grass out from under the snow or to try to find any bushes to eat.

Still far up in the mountains, in much deeper snow, two horses, fighting for their lives, floundered on and on through the girth-deep snow.

It was a wombat, searching food near the river at the first grey, snow-laden dawn, who saw the horses first. A dingo carried the news along the banks of the stream. A kurrawong called it to his mate.

As the daylight grew stronger snow fell less thickly, though the clouds enveloping the mountains told of the blizzard that still raged higher up.

Of the silent, exhausted herd of horses, up near the mouth of the Tin Mine Creek, Koora was the first to start moving around looking for food. She had her foal to feed; she was starving, and there would be no milk for him. She scratched around for grass and the fleshy leaves of a bacon-and-egg bush. Even here the snow was deep, and it was difficult to find anything to eat at all. She looked up the Tin Mine Creek, the way they had come, saw the black clouds, and felt an overpowering fear and desolate loneliness.

Would she never see Thowra, the king, again?

In the Black and Silver Night

The moon was just rising. An unearthly glitter illumined the snow. Shadows of tree or rock moved across the silver world in uttermost silence. A young silver horse, lithe, taut, stood at the top of the cliff that led on to the high plateau. He stood with head thrown up, gazing, feeling. He listened too, but he heard only silence.

He stepped out carefully on the frozen snow. Here, wind and sun, and frost had made a surface like roughened glass.

No mark was made by his hooves – printless, he wove his way through shadow and moonlight. He must hurry, he knew, for he must do what he had to do while the world was frozen hard. He dropped down off the plateau and began to trot along the top of the ridge, along miles and miles of moonlit snow, searching, searching . . . and in all those miles, he saw no sign of life, no mark of bird nor beast on the vast snows.

Presently the ridge began to go upwards again. He slackened his pace till he reached the highest point. There, above five thousand feet, it flattened again, and he trotted on and on, almost due south.

There was a great depth of snow. The landscape had not just been changed by fire: rocks were covered and hollows filled: snow came high up the boles of the trees. The silence was not the silence of death, as it had been after the fire, but everything was indeed strange. No whisper of wind, or of water, or of life broke the absolute quiet.

The young horse stopped for a moment, when the main Quambat Ridge started to drop downwards a little. He stood with one forefoot raised and with ears pricked as though he would hear beyond the frozen quiet, then he turned down a side spur that dropped more steeply and would lead him near to Quambat Flat.

Though the eagles had seemed to lead him, early that day, when he started up from the Murray, none but the moon in the sky saw Baringa trotting over the frost-bound mountains of the south – the land in which, someday perhaps, no stallion would dare challenge him.

Off the top of the ridge the snow had been more sheltered and was covered with two or three inches of frost crystals. Here Baringa did not go printless, and a moon-glowing wake of frost crystals followed each hoof. With rising excitement, he trotted down.

On Quambat Flat there was no sign of another horse, or of any animal at all. It was a great silver plain below the moon and the mountains, below the frost-bright dome of sky – empty, lonely and yet thrilling.

Baringa gazed and gazed at it, and then went on jogging down through the soft swishing crystals. On the edge of the open flat he stood among the black, burnt trees and looked all around very carefully and for a long time, then he could no longer resist the fascination of that great, smooth silver plain

151

which was made for a splendid stallion to gallop on, dance and play.

He cantered out, almost nervously till he was right in the middle, perhaps where the stream ran deeply under snow – a silver horse on the immense silver plain, almost invisible, but he threw a shadow, left a track, flung up a glittering spray of crystals as he burst into a gallop, as he plunged, as he reared, as he sprang into the freezing air.

The moon, the stars, and the mountains looked down on the young horse dancing alone on the great snow-covered space.

At last Baringa stopped. He had come here for a special purpose. He had come because he was consumed with curiosity as to what had happened to Lightning, Goonda and the foal, Cloud, Cirrus, Mist and all the other horses of Quambat, and had seen no one.

He stood quite still, alone in the centre of Quambat Flat – alone and filled with the thrilling excitement of moon-spun snow and the splendidness of being alive.

He raised his head to the moon and the stars, and called a long, loud call. Then suddenly, and from quite close, came an answer, and another, and another. One voice that he knew – or did he? – they echoed so hollowly, round and round. Where did they come from, all those voices? And whose voice had he felt sure he recognised before all the others called and the echoes came? Lightning? Lightning?

He neighed again and listened carefully to echoing, confusing answers. Perhaps they came from near the old stone chimney which still showed above the snow, feathered with ice and rimed with frost. If they were there, the owners of those desperate, echoing voices, he had passed quite close to them. Were they lying, nearly dead with hunger, covered with snow? What had happened? Why couldn't he see them?

He went towards their continued calls, and he went warily, ears pricked, nostrils quivering, yet walking with pride, for this was his hour, in the moonlight and the snow.

As he got closer to where their calls seemed to come from, he thought he saw a line breaking the snow. Then he realised that their neighing echoed, strange and hollow, from *below* the plain.

Thinking there might be some queer trap, he went even more carefully. He paused once when he thought he saw the faintest vapour rising near that line in the snow. Then he went on. Something was moving. Then he saw the milling backs of horses below the level of the snow . . . he could *smell* horses . . . . Then he was standing above them on the brink of a steep, round pit in the snow, and they were staring up at him – sunken-eyed, thin, their coats staring.

Baringa looked at them in amazement.

"However did you all fall in there?" he asked.

"We didn't fall in. The walls have grown round us as we stood together for warmth, and now they have turned to ice. Get us out," Lightning implored. "We have no food, no water."

Baringa looked all round, breathed in deeply and let the air out – a white cloud. Then he looked in again to see who was there. Cirrus, Cloud and Mist were not with them.

"They went down the creek," Lightning answered when he asked where they were. "We should have gone too."

Baringa still could not quite understand how they had become trapped. What was it Benni had said about horses in the snow? Then he remembered. Benni had told him never to huddle in a mob, always keep moving from place to place. A mob beats down the snow where it stands and the walls of snow rise all round and get hard, and the horses are yarded, and there they stand and there they die. This yard of Lightning's had been made even worse by the big freeze.

He shivered. Whatever he did to try to free them, he must not fall in, and he knew that he must start to try to get them out quickly, because he could not bear to stay away from his herd all the next day. Perhaps the weather might change.

"I will move back a bit so that I do not slip in with you, and then I will try to dig, and I will walk to and fro, to and fro, and see if I can break the snow down," he told them and noticed how miserable both Goonda and the foal looked.

"I am so thirsty," she said.

Thirsty and hungry – Koora had been too – Baringa thought. Of course both of them had foals at foot, and he thought, too, of his two silver mares, and was glad he had been able to leave the Canyon without making any tracks. No one should be able to find the way down the cliff.

What would Lightning and the others do if he freed them?

Baringa started to dig with his forefeet. The snow was very hard under its covering of frost crystals, but after all a stallion can dig quite a deep rolling hole in hard earth if he takes some time over it, and Baringa milled around and dug, and even rolled when he got hot. Then he stamped a track to and from the horses' yard, carefully keeping away from the edge.

"Stand on your hind legs and try to break it away a bit yourself," he told Lightning.

Lightning was horrifyingly weak, but he started to work too.

Baringa trampled and dug, trampled and dug.

The moon was beginning to drop lower towards the west but there were still some hours of freeze left. If only he could get them out, dig water for them, and start them off downwards, and then trot as far as the cliff himself, before the sun started to soften the snow, he would be all right.

He looked at the side of the pit where he had been digging and at Lightning breaking it away. Surely they should be able to get out soon – even the foal.

Would Lightning do as he was told, and go down the stream, or would he try to follow him?

Baring stopped his digging and trampling for a moment, and looked over the edge at the horses.

"Lightning," he said. "If I let you out, will you promise me to lead all these horses down the creek and try to find Cloud? You must leave me here. I will look after myself, but I must have your promise that you will go downstream."

"Of course," said Lightning.

Baringa started his digging again.

"If he gets out," he thought, "it will be the third time I have saved him – saved him to plague my mares."

He broke away some more snow. Lightning put his forefeet up and heaved and scrambled, and managed to jump himself out. He was trembling all over.

"Now the foal," said Baringa. "Push him from behind, Goonda."

Long shadows were beginning to fall across the glittering plain as the last horse got out. The moon was sinking. There might be three more hours of frozen snow.

"We must find water," said Baringa, leading the straggling mob down the plain. Each of them threw a long, ragged shadow to the east.

Where he knew there was a bend in the creek, Baringa dug for water. Now, when they had all had a drink, he would tell them to go, and when the last one was out of sight he would turn and go as fast as he could.

154

"Lightning," he said. "You must hurry before the sun thaws the snow. Travel in the freeze again tomorrow night if you do not get far tonight." Then he stood in the last light of the moon, his silver coat spangled with frost crystals, for he had just rolled to free himself of sweat.

"Lightning," he said again. "Will you now cease trying to steal my mares?"

"Mares?" said Lightning.

"Yes, mares," Baringa answered.

"I wouldn't try to steal them," said Lightning, as though he never had tried to take Dawn, and he turned down the river as he had said he would.

Baringa watched them out of sight, knowing that, though he had indeed saved Lightning three times, Lightning would still think, next spring, that because he was older and must be more handsome, Baringa's mares should follow him.

The bright, early sun shone full on to Baringa when at last he reached the top of the cliff. He stood for a moment looking out over his Canyon.

A faint swish and tinkle sounded as the ice-coating on the rocks melted off, slithered and fell. A kurrawong cried in the bright sky. There was life and sound again, not the unearthly silence of the moon-white night and the black shadows and the one young horse alone. But that night had been his, for it was thrilling to travel the frozen world with no other horse, and no other sound. And now he stood in sunshine, the tiredness from his long journey driven out of him by the life-giving power of the sun.

"Thrice have I saved Lightning," he told himself. "It was I who called Steel so that Lightning got away. I led him to safety when he was blind, and now I have freed him from the snow. Surely I shall somehow be able to roam the mountains freely and hold my mares." And he threw up his head in the sunlight and neighed – a call not of pride, but of courage – to the mountains that were empty of horses but were *his* mountains.

His call echoed, echoed off the cliffs and came back to him out of his own Secret Canyon, rolling on and on, and then, as it became faint, a loud, clear neigh answered his.

Baringa turned swiftly. There, poised on another rock above

155

the cliff, mane and tail cascades of silver in the frosty sunlight, stood Thowra, for Thowra and Storm had come up the river, found the herd, and Thowra had come on, seeking Baringa.

They walked to meet each other – the king of the Cascade brumbies and his grandson, the lovely young silver stallion of the south.

Fiction in paperback from Dragon Books

Richard Dubleman
The Adventures of Holly Hobbie   £1.25 ☐

Anne Digby
Trebizon series

First Term at Trebizon   £1.50 ☐
Second Term at Trebizon   £1.50 ☐
Summer Term at Trebizon   £1.50 ☐
Boy Trouble at Trebizon   £1.50 ☐
More Trouble at Trebizon   £1.50 ☐
The Tennis Term at Trebizon   £1.50 ☐
Summer Camp at Trebizon   £1.50 ☐
Into the Fourth at Trebizon   £1.25 ☐
The Hockey Term at Trebizon   £1.50 ☐
The Big Swim of the Summer   60p ☐
A Horse Called September   £1.50 ☐
Me, Jill Robinson and the Television Quiz   £1.25 ☐
Me, Jill Robinson and the Seaside Mystery   £1.25 ☐
Me, Jill Robinson and the Christmas Pantomime   £1.25 ☐
Me, Jill Robinson and the School Camp Adventure   £1.25 ☐

Elyne Mitchell
Silver Brumby's Kingdom   85p ☐
Silver Brumbies of the South   95p ☐
Silver Brumby   85p ☐
Silver Brumby's Daughter   85p ☐
Silver Brumby Whirlwind   50p ☐

Mary O'Hara
My Friend Flicka Part One   85p ☐
My Friend Flicka Part Two   60p ☐

To order direct from the publisher just tick the titles you want
and fill in the order form.   **D8**

Colour illustrated storybooks for the young reader

Help Your Child to Read
Allan Ahlberg and Eric Hill

Fast Frog	85p	☐
Bad Bear	85p	☐
Double Ducks	85p	☐
Poorly Pig	85p	☐
Rubber Rabbit	85p	☐
Silly Sheep	85p	☐

Allan Ahlberg and André Amstutz

Mister Wolf	85p	☐
Travelling Moose	85p	☐
Hip-Hippo Ray	85p	☐
King Kangaroo	85p	☐
Tell-Tale Tiger	85p	☐
Spider Spy	85p	☐

Help Your Child to Count
Richard & Nicky Hales and André Amstutz

Slimy Slugs	95p	☐
Captain Caterpillar	95p	☐
Furry Foxes	95p	☐
Boris Bat	95p	☐
Panda Picnic	95p	☐
Froggy Football	95p	☐

Rub A Dub Dub
Alan Rogers

Yankee Doodle	95p	☐
Three Men in a Tub	95p	☐
One for the Money	95p	☐
Tom, Tom the Piper's Son	95p	☐
Hey Diddle Diddle	95p	☐
Poor Old Robinson Crusoe	95p	☐

To order direct from the publisher just tick the titles you want and fill in the order form.

Fiction in paperback from Dragon Books

Peter Glidewell

Schoolgirl Chums	£1.25	☐
St Ursula's in Danger	£1.25	☐
Miss Prosser's Passion	£1.50	☐

Enid Gibson

The Lady at 99	£1.50	☐

Gerald Frow

Young Sherlock: The Mystery of the Manor House	95p	☐
Young Sherlock: The Adventure at Ferryman's Creek	£1.50	☐

Frank Richards

Billy Bunter of Greyfriars School	£1.25	☐
Billy Bunter's Double	£1.25	☐
Billy Bunter Comes for Christmas	£1.25	☐
Billy Bunter Does His Best	£1.25	☐
Billy Bunter's Benefit	£1.50	☐
Billy Bunter's Postal Order	£1.50	☐

Dale Carlson
Jenny Dean Mysteries

Mystery of the Shining Children	£1.50	☐
Mystery of the Hidden Trap	£1.50	☐
Secret of the Third Eye	£1.50	☐

Marlene Fanta Shyer

My Brother the Thief	95p	☐

David Rees

The Exeter Blitz	£1.50	☐

Caroline Akrill

Eventer's Dream	£1.50	☐
A Hoof in the Door	£1.50	☐
Ticket to Ride	£1.50	☐

Michel Parry (ed)

Superheroes	£1.25	☐

Ulick O'Connor

Irish Tales and Sagas	£2.95	☐

To order direct from the publisher just tick the titles you want
and fill in the order form.

All these books are available at your local bookshop or newsagent, or can be ordered direct from the publisher.

To order direct from the publishers just tick the titles you want and fill in the form below.

Name _____

Address _____

_____

Send to:
Dragon Cash Sales
PO Box 11, Falmouth, Cornwall TR10 9EN.

Please enclose remittance to the value of the cover price plus:

UK 45p for the first book, 20p for the second book plus 14p per copy for each additional book ordered to a maximum charge of £1.63.

BFPO and Eire 45p for the first book, 20p for the second book plus 14p per copy for the next 7 books, thereafter 8p per book.

Overseas 75p for the first book and 21p for each additional book.

Dragon Books reserve the right to show new retail prices on covers, which may differ from those previously advertised in the text or elsewhere.